Columbia
Part I

Tiago Lameiras

Author of *Persephone's Fall*
and *Hypatia: Empress of Alexandria*

Historical Fiction

Columbia

Part 1

Authored & Edited by
Tiago Lameiras

© 2020 Tiago Lameiras

The right of the editor to be identified as the author of the editorial material, and of the author for his individual chapters, has been asserted in accordance with the Copyright Act of 1976 in the United States and sections 77 and 78 of the Copyright, Designs and Patents Act of 1988 in the United Kingdom.

All rights reserved. No part of this book may be reprinted or reproduced or utilized in any form or by any electronic, mechanical, or other means, now known or hereafter invented, including photocopying and recording, or in any information storage or retrieval system, without permission in writing from the publisher.

Columbia: Part I – Edited by Tiago Lameiras.
Includes an index.

Cover Concept by Tiago Lameiras.
«Cantino Planisphere Compass Rose Replica» by Joaquim Alves Gaspar (2011); usage and modification authorized under the provisions of the Creative Commons Attribution-Share Alike 3.0 Unported License and the GNU Free Documentation License (version 1.2 or later).

Printed and bound by Kindle Direct Publishing.

ISBN–10: 1693825961
ISBN–13: 9781693825965

Typeset in Sabon Roman
by Linotype

Columbia, SC, United States

*To Maria, whose heart
is my one safe haven*

"The end of the human race will be that it will eventually die of civilization".

— Ralph Waldo Emerson

Index

Chapter I
On the Lookout for a Paid Partnership 17

Chapter II
Out of Their League 43

Chapter III
The Tables Have Turned 81

Chapter IV
Amphibious Assault 99

Chapter V
Retribution 145

Chapter VI
Land-ho! 183

Chapter VII
Close Encounters of the First Kind 209

Chapter VIII
Los Viajes de Cristóbal Colón 229

Chapter IX
Golden Fever 255

Chapter X
Ayiti 279

Chapter XI
Feliz Navidad 295

Chapter XII
Sling Your Hook 325

DISCLAIMER

This is a work of fiction. Names, characters, businesses, places, events, locales, and incidents are either the products of the author's imagination or used in a fictitious manner. Any resemblance to actual persons, living or dead, or actual events is purely coincidental.

— November 2019

Chapter I
On the Lookout for a Paid Partnership

With barely a little over a month at sea entered in the log after an incident with the rudder of the Pinta – believed by the Admiral to have been sabotaged by her owners, Cristóbal Quintero and Gómez Rascón – and the rigging of the Niña from lateen to the more common square sails while moored at port in the Canary Islands, a mere sixty-two nautical miles off the African coast, though under Spanish rule, Christopher Columbus was facing yet another episode of disobedience, not only from the captains and crew of both caravels, but also the carrack-type he had chosen as the flagship for the enterprise at hand, the «Santa María» – or «La Capitana», as he referred to it –, nearly bordering on classic medieval privateer mutiny, when letters of marque signed by hiring monarchs no longer matter and can easily be discarded by either setting them ablaze (their ashes scattered in the maritime breeze) or simply tearing them apart, leaving the pieces to their disintegrating demise below water. The key difference between a speculative scenario such as this and the actual quagmire Columbus was presently facing was there was absolutely nothing to gain if not the coming of the cloaked skeleton and his scythe, ghastly prepared to reap the hollowed spirits of the men adrift, contrary to treasure chests claimed on behalf of European crowns, despite rarely ever being delivered to them in the end – such was the case with these sailors, most of them formerly imprisoned outlaws, pardoned but not freed (let alone disentangled of their initial fate), as crossing the uncharted Ocean Sea was synonymous with capital punishment, no question about it, but first things first: what was this flotilla doing in the Atlantic to begin with, namely when the calm summer navigation had by now been replaced with possibly dire autumnal weather conditions? Let us look back for a moment.

Beginning in the year four hundred seventy-six, the Roman Empire to the West was dissolved following the fall of its capital, the seven-hill city founded by and named after Romulus about seven hundred and fifty years prior to the birth of the Lord and Savior Jesus Christ, which, in turn, offered several new peoples descending from immigrants based in Britannia, Hispania, North Africa, and Asia a chance to settle across the European continent, eventually ravaging the whole of the Empire and surrounding Rome, which led to the deposition of none other than Flavius Romulus Augustulus, aged sixteen (whose tenure as Augustus had only lasted eleven months), by Odoacer, a Germanic barbarian chieftain who became the first King of Italy. Other areas of the dismantled Roman State were already occupied by: the Suebi and the Visigoths (Iberia); the Vandals (Achaea and Africa – specifically Carthage); the Angles, the Saxons, and the Jutes (Britannia); the Franks (Gallia); the Goths (Tauris and Scandia); the Ostrogoths (Tauris and part of the Italian Peninsula), and the Lombards (the Italian Peninsula). The Huns, who had come from Central Asia, dwelled in Germania for a while, disappearing even before Rome was taken, resulting in the independence of most of the aforementioned peoples; the death of their fierce leader, Attila, contributed a great deal to the weakening of their power.

Some of these regions, of course, did not at all recognize barbarian authority at first, thus remaining loyal to Roman rule, though not for long. Only the Eastern portion of the former Roman Empire, governed by a co-Augustus from Constantinople (originally Byzantium), resisted dissolution for an entire millennium until it fell in the hands of the Ottoman Turks, led by the young Mehmed II in fourteen hundred fifty-three, after a state of siege that lasted just a week short of two full months, officially becoming the new capital of the Ottoman Empire under a brand-new designation – Istanbul. Contrary to Romulus Augustulus, the last Emperor of the East, Constantine XI Palaeologus, gave up his throne by being killed in action.

Southeastern Europe, Asia Minor, and North Africa were now under Muslim control. The safe land routes known to the fairly recent European kingdoms as Silk Roads leading to the Far East, the same Venetian explorer Marco Polo had had the chance to take during his voyages to India, Catayo, and Cipango in the thirteenth century, brilliantly recorded as 'The Travels of Marco Polo' in the year thirteen hundred, were now incredibly deadly to any Christian, thus breaking contact between the two ends of the world, an event that had its toll on European trade expansion and, consecutively, economic growth.

Alternatives needed to be sought, although avoiding the Arabs would prove to be a lot more difficult than initially expected, especially when there were still multiple Muslim strongholds to take over in Europe, particularly in Iberia.

Columbia: Part I

The Kingdom of Portugal had long gotten rid of Arab occupation for good in twelve hundred forty-nine under the command of Afonso III; Castile, however, did not take back its territory completely until the late fifteenth century, when Granada was recovered by both Isabella, Queen of Castile, and Fernando II, King of Aragon, jointly referred to as the Catholic Monarchs, whose union in holy matrimony would contribute to the founding of a unified Spanish State fully supported by the up until then undisputed fervor of Rome, the capital city of a new nation (among several others) succeeding the Kingdom of Italy – the Papal States, spanning all the way to the Republic of Venice, the Duchy of Modena, and Austria to the North, the Grand Duchy of Tuscany to the West, and the Kingdom of Sicily to the South, where a couple of possessions under the Pope's control were also located and enclaved, namely Pontecorvo and Benevento. In turn, San Marino was enclaved by the Papal States, though it always remained under the protection of the Holy See as an independent country.

One other nation found in the Italian Peninsula, specifically to the Northwest, was the coastal Republic of Genoa, whose capital, after which the country took its designation, witnessed the birth of Cristoffa Corombo, the original Ligurian name of the man whose identity kept changing according to the language spoken in the multiple countries he traveled to by sea, having begun to do so around his ten years of age, in the early fourteen hundred and sixties. In plain Italian, as fathered and immortalized by Dante Alighieri in his 'Commedia', he was Cristoforo Colombo; in Portuguese, Cristóvão Colombo; in Spanish, Cristóbal Colón; and finally, in Medieval Latin, the official idiom of Rome spoken all across Catholic Europe by both secular and clerical scholars alike, naturally, he was Christophorus Columbus, directly adapted to English as Christopher Columbus after having docked in both England and Ireland.

Of his four siblings, at least one – Bartholomew – eventually followed his passion for sea traveling and exploration, having both become cartographers while based in the most powerful center of trade in the entire Western world, and that was Lisbon, the capital city of the Kingdom of Portugal and the Algarves. Bartholomew had gone ahead; Christopher then joined him after docking from Ireland in fourteen hundred seventy-seven.

Throughout the following decade, while the Columbus brothers worked on a plan to reach Asia via a westward sea route based on the calculations of a fellow countryman, Paolo dal Pozzo Toscanelli, Christopher settled down and married a Portuguese noblewoman, Filipa Moniz Perestrello, daughter of Bartolomeu Perestrello (of Lombard origin himself), Governor of Porto Santo, the second largest island of the Madeira Archipelago, about two hundred and sixty-eight nautical miles North of the Canary Islands. The wedding took place in the eponymous isle, precisely, just a couple of years after Christopher's relocation, and the couple's first and only child, Diogo Colombo (more commonly referred to as Diego by his father), was born in the beginning of the fourteen hundred and eighties. This knot, however, was not bound to remain tied for too long, as, merely six years in, Filipa perished while still in her twenties.

By then, Christopher had gained a great deal of experience from trading in West Africa, where the Portuguese had founded several settlements and trading posts. Their favorite merchandise were slaves, precious metals such as gold, spices like salt and pepper, and ivory, for which they would offer African empires to the likes of Ghana, Mali, and Songhay cloth, workable metals, modern weaponry, and even fresh water for the irrigation of complex agricultural fields in exchange.

Considering the connections his family in law had with the Lusitanian Crown, together with the services rendered to the King, Columbus finally requested an audience with the sovereign in fourteen hundred eighty-five with the purpose of discussing the plans he and his brother had been brewing up for so long, which, to Christopher's great delight, was granted by the incumbent monarch, João II, the son and successor of Afonso V, who had been presented with a similar proposal himself, authored at the time by Toscanelli. Unfortunately for the latter, the former summarily rejected the plans, putting an end to the ambitions of the Florentine mathematician, eventually delegating his hopes to Columbus and a new king, enthroned just a year before his death in fourteen hundred eighty-two; the Genoese navigator, however, had his own set of demands in mind, which, without much room for surprise, were not questioned by João II, given the hegemony the Portuguese Monarchy was basking in at the time.

Put quite bluntly, Columbus required, first of all, a fully equipped three-ship flotilla for a westbound journey across the Atlantic and back; second, the King was to appoint him «Great Admiral of the Ocean Sea» and Governor of all lands discovered, thus entitling him to ten percent of the total amount of riches obtained on behalf of the Crown as extra collateral. His only obstacle – obtaining accreditation from the King's advisors, which resulted in none other than failure, as Columbus' calculations regarding the Earth's diameter were far inferior than the generally accepted reality, long established by Eratosthenes ever since Antiquity. Suggesting the Earth was flat was purely nonsensical; the works of ancient astronomers and mathematicians, of which Ptolemy was probably the most important, constituted still the main reference for Renaissance scholars, immediately excluding the possibility of a plain in detriment of a sphere. No, the question was computing the correct dimensions and distances based on confirmed readings from the celestial dome, which Ptolemy himself had already done, figuring the Eurasian landmass spanned a total longitude of one hundred and eighty degrees; Columbus, however, based on the readings of Marinus of Tyre, a Phoenician geographer who was a contemporary of Ptolemy and eventually laid the bases of the latter's own works, estimated a longitudinal value of two hundred and twenty-five degrees of land, with a remainder of one hundred and thirty-five degrees covered in water. Should Columbus sail between twenty-five and thirty degrees North of the equatorial line as far as latitude was concerned, the Earth's circumference in this area, according to him, was likely to be around fourteen thousand nautical miles, therefore estimating the distance from Europe to Cipango across the Atlantic at approximately seven hundred leagues, remaining quite confident that traveling from the Azores to the Far East could not at all take much too long, as demonstrated by the readings of Alfraganus (as he was known in the Western world), a ninth-century astronomer from the court of Baghdad, the capital of the Abbasid

Caliphate. Regarding this particular matter, unknown to Columbus, Alfraganus had always made his calculations using the Arabic mile as his default unit of measurement, one the Genoese navigator mistook for the mile used in his own native land ever since the Roman era, which was considerably shorter, leading up to a difference of about eleven hundred and fifty feet; in the end, the actual distance between Europe and Cipango was set at nearly fifty-five hundred and fifty leagues more than Columbus had imagined. Having his venture been deemed unfeasible by the experts and consequently overruled by the monarch, adding to the fact his wife had already passed away into the afterlife, the aspiring maritime explorer had no other reasons to remain in Lisbon; taking the only fruitful result of his short-lived marriage, his son Diogo, Columbus abandoned the Kingdom of Portugal and crossed the border, settling in the center of the Andalusian province, hoping he would be granted an audience with Queen Isabella of Castile, to whom he wished to reveal both his ambitions and intentions fully intact, seeking from the Catholic Monarchs the sponsorship required for what was generally regarded as being no more than a wild goose chase.

As the Moors were defeated and, therefore, pushed further back all the way to the South by the Castilian army against the raging Mediterranean, thus reducing the area of the Emirate of Granada, so did the King and Queen (under whose joint government the innumerous Spanish territories across Iberia were coming together) advance meridionally, establishing their courts and base of operations in the former eponymous capital city of the Emirate, Caliphate, and Taifa of Córdoba. This particular military campaign was as long as the Trojan War – one full decade toward ultimate victory over Muhammad XII's Arabic rule, beginning in fourteen hundred eighty-two.

During this period, Columbus tried to persuade the Catholic Monarchs as much as he possibly could into assessing the proposal he had already presented to the Portuguese Crown. However, because both Isabella and Fernando found it far more important to unify their country first under the Catholic faith and only afterward focus on basking in the economic advantages of trading with the Far East, Columbus' plans were simply put on hold, not discarded. Knowing the future Spanish State would need to financially recover as soon as possible from a lengthy war with the Moors (designated «Reconquista», to be precise), the Queen did not leave Columbus destitute; on the contrary, she provided him an annual pension of twelve thousand maravedis which, in turn, the Italian navigator used to sponsor a local pharmacy run and frequented by his fellow Genoese countrymen.

Forced to wait for the monarchs to advance in their conquering of the last Muslim stronghold in the peninsula, Columbus found the time to upend his personal life as well, especially after befriending Diego de Arana, a Basque. Under this young man's care were his two orphaned cousins, Pedro and Beatriz Enríquez de Arana. Diego was the one responsible for introducing young Beatriz to Christopher, of course, an event soon resulting in an unofficial relationship, despite the latter's ability to remarry on account of widowhood. About a year later, born into this affair was Fernando, named after the King of Aragon and acknowledged by Columbus as legitimate a son as Diogo.

Even though neither his livelihood nor his family's was at stake, the Genoese sailor was not willing to stay put and live out the rest of his time as God's servant on land; Columbus belonged at sea, and that was where they would have to send him to, whichever the cost. Still relying on the Catholic Monarchs' good will, the Italian honored his agreement with Isabella and waited until the very last minaret in Iberia was taken down, ending once and for all Moorish occupation of the peninsula in January fourteen hundred ninety-two; it was then the Queen of Castile granted Columbus yet another audience for the reassessment of his project. Just as it had happened before, however, Her Majesty's advisors were not too keen on supporting the

Columbia: Part I

venture, and not just because of Columbus's misjudgment as far as the science was concerned, but also and especially due to the sum required to fulfill the somewhat risky investment, one the Spanish Crown, ravished by a long-lasting casus belli, did not exceedingly possess. Fortunately for both parties, a great deal of the amount was provided by a banker whose origins the Holy Inquisition targeted above all – the Jewish. His name was Luis de Santángel, the royal treasurer. Even though his family had long converted to Catholicism (at least three generations in the making), they were still branded «conversos», which is to say «converts»; also, not all Jews were willing to give up on their roots so easily, for which reason Crypto-Judaism, as the designation bluntly shows, was still an indoor reality, while simultaneously perpetuating an outlook of the acknowledgement of Jesus Christ as the Son of God and Messiah, instead of the occasional prophet – their resolve earned them the opposite designation of New Christians, which was «Marranos». This was one of the few ways to avoid taking part in the Roman Catholic Church's barbaric public displays – burnings in squares, more commonly, a new cathartic method of teaching the masses of the Western world what could happen to them should they deviate from the path of the righteous, deemed better than Athens' poetic make-believe, celebrated as early as a thousand years prior to this current approach, ironically dubbed «act of faith», as its purpose was none other than salvation through the purging of one's sins in an earthly hellfire.

Santángel put his influence on the royal household to good use and exhorted both Fernando and Isabella regarding the major achievements newly-founded Spain could benefit from should Columbus be successful, a gamble the banker was resolved to believe was the appropriate response to the Genoese sailor's proposal. The King was the first to concede, confident it would lead to fruition; his spouse, however, was yet to be convinced, which is why, at first, Columbus was dismissed from his first audience in years, one which had taken place in the Castle of Alcázar, in Córdoba. Despite their ruling of separate kingdoms, the Catholic Monarchs were indeed giving it their best to present a united front in every sense of the phrase; disagreement was, therefore, not the handsomest of options. Even after so long a belligerent episode, King and Queen had always stayed by each other's side, so why should there be a loose end now, in a time of peace and much needed prosperity? Lisbon did not necessarily have to be the only port of entry to European trade; besides, even if Columbus were to try to sway João II yet again and the Portuguese monarch repeatedly refused to fund the expedition, sooner or later some other

Columbia: Part I

Head of State would probably agree to the Italian's terms, and then what? Would Fernando and Isabella bow like vassals to the taxes imposed by the Kingdom of Portugal when buying spices or slaves, for instance? The fourteen hundred seventy-nine peace Treaty of Alcáçovas was clear – neither the Catholic Monarchs nor the Portuguese King (Afonso V, at the time) would claim the right to take each other's throne, therefore guaranteeing both States' respective independence, together with tolerance and the promise of non-interference; this last part signified that, specifically speaking, any and all Portuguese settlements in Africa or anywhere else belonged to Portugal, which prevented the Spaniards from sailing near such places without previous authorization. Also, the Canary Islands were to remain under Castilian control, as both the Madeira and Azores archipelagos were already enough to cover a long range of travels in any direction, whether the ships in question flew the Portuguese flag or any other from a profoundly multinational Europe, thus generating revenue from both business and tourism, beginning at the seaports. Once these terms were ratified by Pope Sixtus IV in his 'Aeterni Regis' bull two years after the signing of the treaty, there was no turning back. Discrediting the Supreme Pontiff's word was exactly the same as declaring war on God Himself, a hypothetical scenario whose outcome we all know too well; he who turns against the Lord flies with the devil's wings. Then again, there was the issue of a hurting national pride, meaning Portugal had only become a sovereign nation to begin with because of Castile's generosity, acknowledged as such by Alfonso VII, also King of León, in the Treaty of Zamora, signed in eleven hundred forty-three, ratified by His Holiness Alexander III thirty-six years later via his bull, titled 'Manifestis Probatum'. It took Rome that long to award Afonso I of Portugal his royal title and his own kingdom because, throughout these three and a half decades (out of a total four, considering Portuguese independence was declared in eleven hundred thirty-nine), the first monarch of former Portugalia had been busy with his own «Reconquista» campaigns, a demonstration which, judging from a Roman perspective, could only mean he was indeed prepared to be a defender and protector of the One Faith, now paying vassalage directly to the Papal States.

Thusly and in short, Spain was not prepared to lose trading competition to the Portuguese, an important factor that moved Isabella to quickly undo her mistake and send for Columbus immediately and once more as he was preparing to leave Córdoba, if not Spain altogether, desperately taking his projects elsewhere and selling them to the first bidder, given that counting on the highest was not at all suitable, for, at least up until then, no one had shown interest in something as farfetched and uncompetitive as a "Western route to India" and no one likely would, now that Bartolomeu Dias had overcome the infamous Cape of Storms in the Southern tip of the African continent, dubbed by João II «Cape of Good Hope» after the navigator's extraordinary feat, fully clearing the sailing path to Asia and, more importantly, the Indian subcontinent, bathed by the Eastern Ocean (known in Antiquity as the Erythraean Sea). The Catholic Monarchs, in turn, desperately needed to find a way their ships could freely travel through without any special licensing from either neighbors or locals, which is to say a more direct route that did not comprise navigating around an entire landmass or demanding an understanding with local authorities and, who knows, consecutively leading to an unnecessary war overseas with so much trouble to deal with right at home.

No, something else apart from Santángel's money and the loans he had taken himself was required, for which reason a small amount of coercion, if measurable in any way, was definitely involved in the preparation for the event whose conditions were ultimately agreed upon by the monarchs and Columbus in Santa Fé, Granada, three months after the decisive audience; the Queen herself was prepared to pawn her jewels as collateral when taking loans to cover this potentially highly profitable venture, but, in the end, there was no need – it was a question of national interest, so the subjects would just have to help with an extra tax specifically conceived for the fulfillment of the chaptered contract signed with the foreigner. Not only that, given Columbus's nationality, both Genoese bankers living in Seville and Lorenzo il Popolano (or «the Popular», a member of the powerful Florentine House of Medici) were involved in the lending of money.

Apart from the conditions previously established when seeking to convince João II of Portugal, the future Genoese explorer was also able to secure the titles of Governor and Viceroy of any newly-discovered lands, together with «Don», which made him a distinct citizen whose resolve was bound to be acknowledged by the Spanish court; because these pledges were hereditary in their statutes, the Columbian lineage could have just been financially secured in perpetuity from thereon.

All there was left to do now was taking care of the essentials – finding three ships and a crew to distribute across the former, the men being well aware the enterprise on the Queen's behalf might possibly turn out to be no more than a suicide mission, which clearly was not going to be much help once the time came for a little persuasion. In order to quickly take care of this issue, Isabella found an interesting solution – the prerogative of royal indults, instantly freeing criminals from incarceration under the condition they partake in Columbus's mission in the name of the Crown. On the one hand, those without family or a home to get back to regarded the offer as a quicker form of capital punishment, one they had coming anyway due to life imprisonment, which was why not that great a fuss was made; on the other hand, the men who were eagerly waiting for the restoration of their individual rights, consequently hoping to return to their former life, had to face a new trial presided by God Himself, who could either grant them divine clemency by allowing them to come back from the journey or just send them the demon's way and let them die on their path to an uncharted destination. This whole level of uncertainty was too much to bear, even though they did not have other choice but to go along. Nevertheless, it was one thing to embark at gunpoint (or the tip of a blade) and another when left alone at sea, where justice could be taken into one's own hands without much scrutiny. Still, and long before animosity could settle in several hundred leagues into the Ocean Sea, the preparations for said event, while under royal decree, were merely stirring the pot toward general misdemeanor from the people of Palos de la Frontera, Andalusia (about sixty miles West-southwest of Seville, where the Odiel River flows straight into the Gulf of Cádiz and, soon after, the Atlantic), as many refused to serve the foreign navigator and grant him the necessary provisions for survival aboard the three ships yet to be chosen, unquestionable evidence of a nationalist spirit coming together after the defeat of infidel invaders, even though the latter saw it the other way around – at least as far as faith was concerned, anyway.

Time was at a premium, constituting a luxury Columbus could not afford for too long, or he and his prospective crew would soon face the most dangerous period of the Ocean Sea typhoon season, undoubtedly risking their lives even worse than peacefully moving westward beyond a point of no return to the safety of European ports – this is why choosing fast, sleek ships was paramount. Unable to sweep the Southern coastline in search for the best vessels, Columbus had no other choice but to make do with what was locally available, and he absolutely did not regret it, for he eventually found a promising trio capable of performing the task at hand.

Moored in Palos de la Frontera was a nearly fifty-year-old caravel (originally a Portuguese invention whose development, under Henrique the Navigator's sponsorship, was essential for the continued exploring of Sub-Saharan Africa, especially once they became rigged with lateen sails and the rudder was placed in the center, therefore increasing maneuverability) popularly referred to as «La Pinta», property of Cristóbal Quintero and Gómez Rascón in early fourteen hundred ninety-two. Cristóbal, along with his brother, Juan, descended from a family of sailors and shipowners. Their cousins, the Niños of Moguer (located about five miles Northeast of Palos de la Frontera), also partook in the business, being the proud owners of the Santa Clara, dubbed «La Niña» among local mariners on account of the owners' family name and moored next to the Pinta. It is fair to say the Niña was probably Columbus's love at first sight, for it was slightly smaller than the Pinta, definitely not as heavy and, more importantly, gifted with a design that made her far more hydrodynamic than her cousin, though her actual speed test was yet to come, once her lateen sails were swapped in order to increase her performance while sailing in open sea; the fact it had been built with three masts only made the Genoese covet the vessel even more. Both ships were soon commissioned by port authorities under royal decree, which predicted a maximum of ten days for the acquisition of crafts, crew, and supplies; this short amount of time, however, was dilated to over two months, as the resistance to this foreign would-be Admiral who had managed to garner the Catholic Monarchs' complete trust was much too difficult to fight off. Not only that, the

Italian navigator was still one ship short of the magnificent trio Isabella and Fernando had agreed to concede him for this experimental journey.

Neither the Pinta nor the Niña were large enough to accommodate food, drink and still protect the men from the burning Sun during daylight and the cold-freezing Moon at night. The best option for those joining Columbus (officers such as the masters and the captains included) was to just find a spot on deck between shifts and lie down on the wooden planks, looking to grab a wink while others were right by their side, either at work, eating, drinking, talking, chanting, or simply relieving themselves in shared buckets to be regularly thrown overboard and lifted back up for continued usage, washed and disinfected with the help of salt water.

All of these cons naturally constituted an obstacle as far as recruiting seamen was concerned. Columbus, of course, would not subject himself to the same conditions; he was in charge of the enterprise and the flotilla was his to command, for which reason he required a flagship of his own choosing where he would carry a larger amount of supplies, more men (among which those working directly for him would feature, from his servant and ship's boy to the royal secretary of the flotilla) and, unsurprisingly, a roof over his head, which is to say a poop deck with his personal windowed

Columbia: Part I

cabin just below located in the stern section (the aftercastle), sheltering him from the noise, the smell, and the impending weather, regardless of how delightful it could get. It would be unfair to say the senior crew did not have a place of their own for just a wee bit of privacy, and that is why the forecastle in the bow must not be forgotten; juniors, on the other hand, would have to make use of the single deck in between.

Anchored at the port of Palos de la Frontera, only one ship featuring these commodities was found – the Santa María, otherwise known as «La Gallega», owned and captained by Juan de la Cosa; it was not a caravel, but rather a carrack or, as the Portuguese would call it, a "nau", bearing a bowsprit which allowed a further forward location of the foremast in the hull and the securing of a foresail to the craft.

And so it was that, after much negotiation with hundreds of people all at once, Columbus obtained his three ships, the necessary resources for all the men to stay alive for at least a few weeks, and the crewmembers themselves, totaling about ninety (forty aboard the Santa María, captained by de la Cosa, twenty-six on the Pinta, captained by Martín Alonso Pinzón, and twenty-four on the Niña, captained by the latter's brother, Vicente Yáñez Pinzón), the whole squadron making their way from Palos de la Frontera, mainland Spain, on the third of August, fourteen hundred ninety-two, hoping to find the Eastern tip of the Asian continent as described by Marco Polo and, consequently, make naval and world history.

As a reward from Queen Isabella, the first to sight land would be entitled to a yearly ten thousand-maravedi pension for life, and that was more than enough for all sailors to keep their eyes wide open; the problem was, given only one man could claim the prize, the majority was not at all interested in risking their lives in mare incognitum for too long while bearing in mind singular contentment. It was up to Columbus to reassure everyone the enterprise would eventually pay off, but, as time kept flying by, carried by the ocean breeze on its lap, so did the patience of the many, outweighing the will power of the one – the Admiral, who, in spite of being the leader of the flotilla, he did not have the right to overstep the shipmaster's boundaries and take control of the vessel. However, since Columbus outranked de la Cosa, the Genoese officer of the royal navy progressively took over all three ships, piloting the Niña and the Pinta from La Capitana. Morally damaged because of Columbus's failure to mind his own business in the aftercastle, de la Cosa, the Pinzón brothers, and the other seamen in general (their main reasons being rotten food, scarce freshwater, exhaustion, and disease – scurvy and insolation, especially) felt like humbling the Admiral just enough to relieve him of his authoritarian command.

Chapter II
Out of Their League

On the first Sunday of October, fourteen hundred ninety-two (either by sheer coincidence or, as was soon to be observed by the majority of the ninety men aboard the flotilla, a heavenly sign), the seventh day of the month (precisely when the Lord took His rest after having seen that it was all good), a harquebus round was fired by an officer from the foremost vessel, the fastest of the trio, the Niña, captained by Vicente Yáñez Pinzón, reverberating like a ripple on the Ocean Sea's surface within earshot of both La Capitana and the Pinta, as Columbus had previously instructed all ships were to stick close during key moments throughout the day, especially at dawn and dusk, when the mist cleared the most and the best eyes among the crew could physically scout for land up to approximately twenty nautical leagues ahead. This had been the reason, precisely, for the Niña to sound the alarm at sunrise, additionally hoisting the royal standard all the way up to the masthead for visual confirmation – Vicente Yáñez Pinzón had strong motives to believe the venture was finally going to pay off after innumerous other sightings which, eventually, turned out to be nothing more than frustration, progressively making room for the buildup of anger in the hearts of the mariners, thus dimming any chances of an increase in morale.

The life of one man alone among nine-dozen others could suddenly change as long as he lived; were he careful enough not to spend it all at once on frivolities, he would at least be able to return to Spain and make a comfortable living without having to loiter the excrement-paved streets, engaging in something as vital as begging for a loaf of bread and a ladle of soup water, sooner or later succumbing to the soulless withdrawing powers of death by either malnourishment, disease, or both. Not to be unnecessarily repetitive (even though one may surreptitiously yield to said temptation), but not all of the seamen joining Columbus were social castaways, of course; there were those of an unshakable reputation that required the most thorough of cares, with a family to support, a business to run…

in short, a household whose head could not afford to stain his respective coat of arms. All these reasons were sufficiently valid to yearn for compensation while risking one's life on behalf of the Crown, therefore rendering the crew extraordinarily excited to spot any natural element at all that could indicate the presence of a floral horizon not too far from the flotilla's position, allowing them to temporarily abandon ship, set their feet on land, bathe in freshwater, drink it (not in that particular order, of course), collect whichever perishables they could find and, lastly, let the Admiral come along with people who actually wanted to join him in their stead, never having to deal with an arrogant foreigner again.

The general mood across all three ships bore a somewhat wavy pattern, meaning it kept fluctuating up and down, even though the tendency was, nevertheless, to wander below an imaginary line of acceptance; we can only suppose it is true what those of an elderly age say after all, that a one-time grievance easily deposes frequent acts of compassion toward another. Then again, the only person in the situation at hand who was capable of summoning such a quality (should he want to) was Columbus, and he obviously was not in it for the altruistic side of things; this was his project, years of planning were at stake, regardless of how miscalculated they might have been. The Admiral was not really willing to part with his records until he could show them to Their Majesties as supporting evidence of the existence of a westward route to India; not just that, he was the only one who had chambers of his own, the sort he could enjoy with all the privacy a regular sailor had no choice but to simply dream of; the remaining officers slept under the foredeck and in the forecastle, no less, though it was communal. Columbus did the readings based on both a sunny day and the starry night sky via the use of a quadrant, while the men were too busy gnashing their teeth of either heat, cold, rage, thirst, hunger, or all of those combined, for which reason they were much too busy to keep track of the actual distance traveled up until that first week of October; still, that did not mean Columbus was above being outsmarted by far more experienced seamen than the lookouts up in the crow's nests of the entire vessel trio.

Once the crew of the Niña realized they had all been the victims of yet another blunder, the ship's Captain, Yáñez Pinzón, gave his sailors the order to furl the sails halfway until the Santa María could catch up, so he could present the Admiral his intentions to board La Gallega and converse with him about both his and the men's displeasure regarding the ongoing circumstances of this incessantly ill-advised journey. With his arms crossed in front of his chest and a frowny look provoked by

Columbia: Part I

both daylight and mild rage, Yáñez Pinzón was waiting atop the poop deck as the Santa María's bowsprit steadily sailed along the calm surface, the Pinta following close behind. Once the Captain figured it was no longer necessary to strangle his already sore throat by calling out on the Admiral while shouting, he approached the taffrail, rested the palms of his hands on the wooden structure and sought to address the ship's boy and personal servant to Columbus, Pedro de Salcedo, who had joined his master not long before, warning him of the hypothetical sighting of land, soon leaving him once more after the blunder to tend to other affairs on behalf of the senior crew, gathered in the forecastle; he was just crossing the midships and about to knock on the door, when Yáñez Pinzón whistled and, having caught his attention, said:

'Salcedo! Go fetch the Admiral and tell him I'm requesting permission to come aboard! I need to discuss a few matters with him before we move along any further'.

The boy nodded and bowed to the Captain's will, smartly coming about and heading back the nearly seventy feet of open deck, dodging those washing, eating, and relieving themselves on it, some of which made a game of testing just how far their urine would go up on the floor, shooting against the wind, just so they could let the ones taking care of the cleaning they had missed a few spots, eventually enraging and igniting a brawl among them all, had the ship's captain and master, Juan de la Cosa, not intervened, though with a double purpose, first saying:

'Hey! Knock it off, you hedge-born skamelars! Get back to your swabbing! And you two pissants join them! You wet it, now mop it!', adding afterward, on a lower register, 'Salcedo, what did the Captain want?'.

The ship's boy promptly responded:

'Captain Pinzón would like a word with the Admiral, sir. He requests that he board the ship, so business may be conducted', Salcedo concluded, expounding his eloquence, one he was working on as the mindful servant of Columbus, a self-taught polyglot and geographer, knowledgeful enough to convince Her Majesty, Queen Isabella of Castile, to fund an expedition every European academic had vouched against on the grounds of unshakable unfeasibility.

Deliberately ignoring the boy's words at a silver maravedi each, de la Cosa posed a series of outraged questions:

'Why in God's plan did Pinzón tell you to ask Colón if he could board my ship?! Am I not the Captain of this vessel? Am I not her master?! Does the foreigner also get to tell him which days of the week he can come by my house and take my wife?! Come about and tell Pinzón that he if he wants to set foot on my livelihood, he needs to ask Captain de la Cosa. Savvy, Salcedo?!'.

Despite being Columbus's personal aide, Salcedo was in fact, let us stress it yet again, the ship's boy, for which reason he did not have much choice but to obey commands from every officer, either relaying messages or delivering rolls of parchment across bow and stern, respectively running fore and aft, trying not to slip overboard due to strong weather activity along the way. Somewhat confused about the proper thing to do, eventually yielding to de la Cosa for fear of being charged with insubordination, Salcedo turned around and was ready to approach the taffrail of La Gallega by the middle (given she had already caught up with the Niña), close to the stairs leading down from the quarterdeck on the starboard side in order to announce the demands of one captain to another. Because of de la Cosa's infuriated crescendo, however, Columbus opened the door to his cabin, lodged all the way aft, and came out, only to immediately face the ship's master and ask of him:

'What's with all the ruckus, de la Cosa? Why are you yelling so close to my quarters?'.

The use of the possessive pronoun in that second question only contributed to an even more riled up captain, master, both or... just neither, as per the Admiral's sincerest viewpoint – one he did not care to hide, flaunting it as frequently as possible, for that matter.

De la Cosa was prepared to share a piece of his mind regarding the self-proclaimed «Don» Cristóbal, when the voice of the latter drew Salcedo back up the stairs again and onto the quarterdeck, where he briefly explained to his utmost master what all the ado was about, basically ignoring de la Cosa's authority, as per his primary job description. The moment the boy finished, Columbus, who had in the meantime placed his knuckles on both sides of his waist, quickly turned his eyes to de la Cosa and, taking yet another chance to belittle that foolishly petty man, gave Salcedo new orders, his gaze still meeting de la Cosa's:

'Inform Captain Pinzón he is most welcome to board us – on my authority, just as he requested'.

'Aye, sir', Salcedo quickly replied, happy to leave the two officers on their own, juggling an icy tension between them, broken only by Columbus's return to his cabin. A few sailors had stopped to pay attention to the minor conflict, impatiently waiting for the captain de jure (demoted to de facto by the Admiral) to throw a hook at him, eventually disappointing themselves. De la Cosa's facial expression and body language hinted without a doubt his blood was dangerously nearing its boiling point, making him want to kick down the door to a cabin that was originally his, but he ended up backing down in an ironically paradoxical figure of speech, quickly turning around to face portside, where the Pinta sailed at roughly the same speed as La Gallega. Up in her poop deck was the other Pinzón brother, Martín Alonso, busy with a few calculations distributed across the top of a desk he worked upon before the Sun started hitting too hard on his skin and through the punctured waistcoat and sweaty shirt a few rodents seemed to have already nibbled on for a while.

De la Cosa did not even notice his men facing the other way the moment he turned around himself, as they pretended they had not stopped working just to witness the potential result of a fight brewing in the long-forgotten horizon where the firmness of the Canary Islands could once be seen. He considered calling upon Alonso Pinzón for a moment, but figuring he was so focused on whatever it was he was doing, de la Cosa chose to climb up the stairs to the poop deck of his own ship, waiting for the right time to drop on his eaves – and not just literally, no; the Genoese's leapfrogging had to be paid for, were he lucky enough to survive the trip back to Castile, a requirement a great deal of seamen aboard the flotilla had no choice but to meet in order to press charges and judicially act against Columbus in a court of law whose trial should be directly presided by Their Majesties. It was something to think about and, most assuredly, at some point in time eventually crossed de la Cosa's mind, though, then again, it would be much easier to sign a blood pact with the sailors, put the foreigner in chains and throw him overboard with a weight strapped to his feet; such was the privateer way and yet they sailed on, providing no one with a single drop of satisfaction whatsoever but themselves. It was the liberal artists and the royal stewards and secretaries who presented a fair obstacle in an otherwise perfect plan.

While the supposed captain of La Gallega paced with a slight hunch on the poop deck fore and aft as his hands were holding each other behind his back, ruminating over a set of innumerous possibilities on how to legitimately make Columbus the bad guy and get rid of him with or without legal proceedings involved, Pedro de Salcedo asked both Antonio de Cuéllar, a carpenter, and López, a joiner, for help with the proper board to place between the deck of the Santa María and that of the Niña, so Yáñez Pinzón could board the former and have his desired word with the Admiral in his quarters.

As the sailors aboard the Niña tried their best to keep her side by side with the Santa María, whose draft was considerably higher than the former's (by a little over three feet, given La Gallega's hull was necessarily larger, in order to store the majority of provisions and other effects), the three

Columbia: Part I

men on the smooth sailing flagship made sure the plank was steady enough for Yáñez Pinzón to safely cross the open sea gap between one vessel's midships section and the other, where there was no taffrail – a dangerous naval feature (or lack thereof), particularly should there be a storm brewing in the middle of God-knows-where, for none of those ninety souls surely knew (nor did the sage masters back in Europe, for that matter).

The moment Yáñez Pinzón approached, Pedro de Salcedo promptly bowed in deference to the Captain, greeted and asked of him:

'Good morrow, Captain. Please follow me. The Admiral awaits you in his quarters'.

'Thank you, Salcedo', he replied, immediately adding, 'oh!, by the way – was de la Cosa posing any problems earlier, when I asked to come aboard? It seemed to me like he wasn't too keen on the idea... then again, the wind wouldn't let me hear straight'.

'Erm...', Salcedo began to utter, trying his best to come up with a valid excuse, 'no, sir; he was just admonishing a few men on account of their misdemeanor. Not to worry, though – Master de la Cosa is more than happy to have you on the Santa María', the servant concluded as both of them climbed up the stairs on the starboard side to the quarterdeck, which very much worked as Columbus's personal cuddy, meaning an open-air antechamber.

Still in response to Salcedo's little white lie and after observing de la Cosa's pensive posture, who seemed to be completely unaware of his presence (considering he was turning his back on the entire vessel), Yáñez Pinzón said:

'Aye... I'm sure he is'.

Little did the Niña's Captain know de la Cosa was in fact mustering his every focusing skill so he would not miss a thing from that meeting. To his knowledge, La Gallega was still his property and nobody was going to take her away from his calloused seaman hands – enough was enough.

Pedro de Salcedo knocked on the cabin's door twice, opened it without waiting for verbal consent from Columbus and stepped forward, reporting the following:

'Admiral, Captain Yáñez Pinzón is here to see you'.

'That's fine, Salcedo. You can go', the Genoese replied, busy measuring his charts, the soft sound of friction between pieces of parchment projecting wisdom across the four corners of the quarters.

'Aye, sir. Captain, if you will', the ship's boy said, addressing the Niña's highest-ranking officer as he stood next to the door, clearing the entrance for the Admiral's visitor.

Yáñez Pinzón did not miss his cue and walked in, swapping places with Salcedo, who bowed and left, gently closing the door behind him and leaving

Columbia: Part I

the two men to their privacy in a noble-like fashion, something which did not go unnoticed by Yáñez Pinzón.

'I'll be damned, Colón…! It seems like you've been feeding royalty to this boy. He's come a long way since you took him for a lackey', the Captain jestingly pointed out.

'Why would that surprise you, Pinzón…? I'm the Admiral of the Fleet, appointed by the Queen herself, who happened to agree to make me "Don Cristóbal", which is the kind of reverence I'd expect from you, especially when you're standing on my deck', Columbus retorted, putting the man in what he thought was his rightful place without looking up and facing him not even once amid his calculations.

Meanwhile and directly above, Juan de la Cosa was not pacing fore and aft anymore. In, fact he could not be seen unless someone went up the foredeck and deliberately looked for him; it just so happens he was in a prone position, almost as if he were fused to the poop deck's boards themselves. Even though he kept the Santa María well maintained, given he was her usual master and captain, the vessel was aging; not only that, sailing on salt water contributed heavily to her further corrosion – the hull most of all, of course, but the wind made sure the entire wooden structure got chewed on, one way or another, which meant a few cracks, no matter how small and thin, had begun to appear in the most assorted places. Fortunately for de la Cosa, and despite the wear and tear of his breadwinner, one of those cracks was on the cabin's roof, which made it easier for the ship's master to eavesdrop, instead of pulling a stunt such as hanging overboard from the taffrail with one of his ears pasted to the thick glass of one of the four windows – it would have been much too dangerous to do so, and God only knows what kind of creatures lurked below the apparently innocent Ocean Sea surface... what if they took him for bait and ate him in one bite? And what if those creatures were sea pigs with sharp teeth, or maybe a polypus with pinching and crushing claws or, worst of all, possibly, a siren...? Not to mention whales, of course, the same beast sort of beast that had swallowed Jonah whole, precisely. It is true the biblical character was saved in the end, but de la Cosa was not planning on risking being trapped in an animal's stomach for a split second, let alone three full days – even if he too found dry land in the aftermath. No, the voyage was risky enough as it was, for which reason he could do without the antics; God needed not be provoked any further.

He covered his other ear with his hand and sought to focus exclusively on the conversation taking place down below, one that was already making his blood boil right from the start (such

Columbia: Part I

was Columbus's gift), for the Admiral's claim Yáñez Pinzón was standing on "his" deck was beyond insulting to de la Cosa as shipmaster and owner. Then again, the "reverence" the Admiral demanded the Niña's Captain take when addressing him was not at all a page-turner as far as the latter was concerned, making him think de la Cosa might be onto something regarding his attitude over the last few weeks, which is why Yáñez Pinzón decided to counter-attack and corner Columbus by picking up the conversation from his remark about Pedro de Salcedo:

'Speaking of "long way", Don Cristóbal', Yáñez Pinzón said in a derisive tone, 'would you care to explain to me, with the help of your endless wisdom and sea savvy', he added, his voice in a crescendo as he went for the finish, 'why is it we're nearly two hundred and fifty leagues above your projections and still no land is in sight?! We've traveled an extra eight hundred and sixty miles, and you know why?! Because you don't know where we are and now it's too late to turn around!'.

It was at this moment in time Columbus dropped his compass and nearly tore his maps with the tip of his ink-soaked quill, as the inkwell also threatened to tip and permanently scar the parchment with blots. Not only that, the Admiral faced Yáñez Pinzón with a look in his eyes that would easily make anyone think there might be an actual fire raging in his irises.

'Ah!... I see I've gotten your attention... Colón', the Captain of the Niña remarked with a lower voice register, stressing the Admiral's family name enough to make him realize he was but a commoner like everybody else involved in the enterprise; in doing so, he also crossed his arms in front of his chest, defensively, waiting for Columbus to provide a logical explanation to his perversely double-crossing actions.

'What are you talking about, Pinzón...? Where did you get that absurd an idea?!', the Admiral asked, standing upright from his desk and quickly running to the Niña's Captain to hold him by his collar, immediately resuming his firing in an enraged whisper face to face with the former, 'Have you been spreading this sort of lies to your men?! Is your brother in on it too?! Have you any idea how long I've waited for this journey to come true?! I know what you're all trying to do, but it won't work! Oh!, no...', he said, pausing to look the Captain in the eyes, his own shimmying uncontrollably, after which he added, 'listen to me carefully, Pinzón - I assure you there'll be hell to pay if I so much as dream you or anyone else is attempting to ruin my one chance at success, capisce?!'.

'Get your dirty seadog paws off me, Colón!', Yáñez Pinzón aggressively told Columbus, jetting

Columbia: Part I

his hands away, pushing him back a couple of steps and, finally, adjusting his shirt, which was already wrinkled and messed up, anyway, but still – there was a question of honor to observe; Yáñez Pinzón was then the one advancing, holding his right index finger to the Admiral's face, both calmly and assertively adding, 'You may have been appointed by the Queen as the man in charge, but you don't have the authority to endanger the lives of nearly a hundred others! We're at a point of no return, Colón. The food is rotting and infested with maggots, our freshwater is down to drops, the men are peeling from sunburn… some of them are even riddled with scurvy because we can't eat that putrid fruit we're carrying and sooner or later we'll have to throw it in the water!'.

Columbus stared at him with his mouth half-opened, his shoulders slightly raised and rigidly held in place together with his arms extended through the length of his upper torso, also somewhat hardened; his breathing was labored, though not too loud. In turn, Yáñez Pinzón had started to pensively pace left to right and back, eventually stopping portside to face the cabin window, whose thick glass produced an indiscernible picture. He resumed talking, turning midsentence from where he was to look at Columbus yet again:

'There's only one thing to do… if we turn around now, we might still make it alive to the

Azores and, whichever island we happen to find first, we lay anchor, unload and head for the shore. Hopefully, we'll have enough strength left to row to the beach, restock, and go home'.

Yáñez Pinzón eventually saw a look of despair combined with rage in the Admiral's visage, but the latter's folly could not go on at the expense of so many people, regardless of them having a home to go back to or not. The Captain of the Niña was now walking to the cabin door and about to grab the knob to open it and leave, when Columbus impulsively ran for it and slammed his entire bodyweight against it as if he were there lying on it, only vertically. Yáñez Pinzón could not help but hop from all the ruckus, also rendered confused by the apparatus, soon after stating in a crescendo:

'What in God's name are you doing, man?! Out of my way!'.

'I'm sorry, Pinzón, but you're not leaving my quarters until we settle this', said Columbus, hypnotically.

'What...?! Oh!, Christ... you've gone insane, haven't you? It's because we've been at sea this long, isn't it? The damned hunger's made you feeble-minded', Yáñez Pinzón observed, actually feeling a tad sorry for the Admiral – until he decided to open his mouth again, that is.

'Far from it, Pinzón... my mind's never been clearer', Columbus replied, slowly stepping away

Columbia: Part I

from the cabin door and approaching the Captain of the Niña with an eerie glistening in his eyes, adding, 'the mist we've been sailing into each morning is the direct result of proximity to land, don't you see?! You're an experienced seaman, you know how it works…! The fog that creeps onto the shore is the exact same one we navigate through on the surface – that's where it comes from! We're this close, Pinzón, this close!', the Admiral remarked, gesturing how short a distance they all were from changing the course of History.

Yáñez Pinzón remained silent, half-opening his mouth soon after to counter Columbus' statement, but the Admiral went on:

'Do you really want to turn your back on a gold mine just waiting there for us…? We'll all be set for life, once we establish a direct sea route from Spain to Cipango, then Catayo, then India! The Portuguese are taking forever going around the whole of Africa, hombre! It took Marco Polo himself three years to get there via the Silk Road! We've only been at sea a little over a month… it'll be the greatest feat ever accomplished! How can you possibly refuse a chance like this, Pinzón?! Especially now that we've come this far!', the Admiral finished in contagious excitement.

Yáñez Pinzón was not exactly sure what to say after having listened to that remarkably compelling argument, which is why his first few utterances were:

'I... I must be the crazy one', he said, burying his face in his right hand while the left rested on his hip on the same side; he was also unable to hold back a bit of a scoff, given how ridiculously easy he had been swayed by the Admiral into changing his opinion in less than a minute.

'It makes sense, doesn't it, Pinzón?', Columbus vivaciously asked the man, somewhat hunching in order to look him in his eyes, hidden behind his fingers with a slight touch of embarrassment.

The Captain of the Niña eventually resurfaced from the palm of his right hand, placed it on his right hip and, looking quite symmetrical, took a deep breath and ended up nodding, a sign of approval to which he added:

'Fine. You had yourself a deal... it's still on'.

Columbus was about to joyfully run to and hold him with the words "thank you" already rolling out of his tongue, but Yáñez Pinzón was not yet done and made the Admiral halt on the tip of his toes when he said:

'However – if we can't find any other evidence on which to rely as proof there is in fact land somewhere around these parts in a couple more days, I will come about and take with me whoever wants to leave... savvy?'.

Having been so assertive and convincing only a few moments before, Columbus felt deep in his

Columbia: Part I

innards he was bartering with a man much too smart for his own sake, but the truth is it was better to have that same man keep his mouth shut for a little longer than the thought of either him being relieved of his command, or simply left alone at sea – quite possibly on a rowboat, with no food or water to hold his soul to his body under the scorching Sun; regarding the deserters' explanation as to why he was gone once they were summoned by the Catholic Monarchs, they would most likely tell Their Graces he had not made it on account of dehydration, his corpse thrown in the sea for the sake of public health and eventually turned into polypus fodder, thus irretrievable. All of this came to Columbus in what felt like a fraction of a second to him, though he had taken his sweet time to answer Yáñez Pinzón's counterproposal:

'Aye… aye, you got it!', the Admiral finally uttered, bearing a disturbing smirk on his face as he spoke with his jaws clenched.

Just after both men honored their mutually beneficial compromise by holding each other's right forearm, there was a knock on the door from Pedro de Salcedo, who did not walk in as before, for the Admiral's new visitors had yet to be announced, given their unexpected presence on the quarterdeck.

The thing is, once de la Cosa heard the part of the conversation during which Yáñez Pinzón was preparing to leave the cabin and announce to the men his resolve to turn around, the former swiftly arose, ran down the stairs to the quarterdeck and asked Martín Alonso Pinzón, the Captain of the Pinta, if he could come aboard, for he had something of the utmost importance to relay to him. There being no objections, de la Cosa took hold of a relatively heavy wooden plank all alone and, without caring for any of the formalities he had demanded himself everybody else observe regarding the Santa María, put the platform in place, let it fall on the Pinta's midships deck with a bang and ran across it, quickly boarding the vessel. Needless to say Alonso Pinzón was far from impressed by de la Cosa's recklessness, but he considered there were much more important things to be concerned about, for which reason he did not approach the subject when the Santa María's shipmaster nearly flew in his direction.

'Pinzón', he began, simultaneously trying to catch his breath, 'your brother boarded my ship only a while ago and...', he stopped, sighing while he found support for his hunching with his hands on his knees, finally proceeding uninterruptedly, 'and he told Colón he's had enough, that going

Columbia: Part I

over by two hundred and fifty leagues is unacceptable and that he's coming about, hoping to find the Azores before we're all done for'.

Alonso Pinzón's facial expression quickly changed from unappreciation to disturbing surprise, especially once de la Cosa mentioned the number of leagues they had all sailed over the agreed upon limit. He swiftly grabbed his own inkwell, placed it atop his charts so they would not fly away in case of a gust, and took a step forward, closing in on the distance between him and de la Cosa, eerily asking the latter:

'Exactly how long have you known we're far beyond Colón's predictions...?'.

The Santa María's master and often commander was rendered somewhat confused, an unasked for favor he returned to the Pinta's Captain:

'Well – how long have you known we're far beyond Colón's predictions?!'.

'I got my confirmation only a while ago. I trusted Colón and didn't bother doing the arithmetic myself, but once I realized our resources were getting scarce, I crammed up the charts and started doing some measurements. It turns out my numbers, while different from Vicente's, aren't that far behind. Now, answer the question – how long have you been sitting on this information, Juan? You're in collusion with Colón, aren't you? We keep pushing forward until all of our dead bodies are thrown in the sea so you and the self-proclaimed Admiral can split the Queen's reward, isn't that right?!'.

'What?! Are you out of your mind?!', de la Cosa asked him, incredulity spread all over his face, after which he explained, 'I'm fed up with Colón! I can't even look the man in his face, Pinzón! He's expropriated me of everything I own! He put himself in charge of my ship, he's giving my crew direct orders... he's even kicked me out of my own quarters! That cabin is my second home, Pinzón. It's my personal sanctuary... currently occupied by a foreign churl!'.

'Well, if he's taken over, why did you let him to boot, man?!', Alonso Pinzón asked of him, to which he replied:

'Because I am but one, Pinzón. The men aren't happy about having him boss them around, either, but what are they going to do? Most of them don't even know each other, and there's simply a lot of nobility on deck. Turning against Colón is turning against the Queen – what do you think will happen once we get back? We'll be either set on fire alive or with a broken neck; one way or another, we certainly won't get a chance to tell the tale. We must either present a united front and get him in chains on the grounds of insanity, or keep wandering about until there's no one left to commandeer either of these vessels. Are you with me, Pinzón? And more importantly – is your brother with us?'.

Columbia: Part I

Alonso Pinzón remained pensive for a while as he ogled all across de la Cosa's visage, then turning starboard to face the cabin where Columbus and his brother, Yáñez Pinzón, were having a heated argument – to the best of de la Cosa's knowledge, that is. The Captain of the Pinta then faced the master of the Santa María once more and asked him:

'Isn't your master-at-arms somehow related to Colón?'.

'Yes', de la Cosa replied, 'I mean, he's not my master-at-arms, he's Colón's mistress's cousin… they're basically family, so he'll definitely stand by his side and will require shackling – good thinking, Pinzón; we'll throw them both in the hull'.

'Before we do, however, I'd like to hear my brother's thoughts on the matter. We'll bring the crew in on this only if we run out of options, otherwise… chaos will be inbound and all the officers will end up in chains at the hands of the help', Alonso Pinzón remarked, seeking to dim hostilities to a minimum, completing his train of thought with the words, 'let's move out'.

The Captain of the Pinta went on ahead while de la Cosa momentarily fell behind, unsure of that somewhat merciful posture shown by the former, though he ended up tacitly agreeing to it, considering it was his best shot at regaining command of his own vessel. As it turns out, Columbus and de la Cosa had a great deal more in common than they thought, even though their wishes in this particular case were quite the opposite of each other.

Both men did indeed move out and boarded the Santa María, and it was not just her crew that was beginning to gain interest in further developments – on the contrary, all sailors from all three vessels were growing all the more suspicious as the chain of command's top entities gathered in the Admiral's cabin; as to what avail, that was yet to be figured out. As Alonso Pinzón and de la Cosa headed aft toward the quarterdeck, Antonio de Cuéllar and López retracted the plank the Santa María's master had extended himself to reach the Pinta, eventually discussing between them what all that could be about, beginning with the joiner:

'What do you suppose is going on here, then?'.

'I've no idea', Cuéllar replied, 'but I've a feeling the worst of this journey has yet to come... you seldom see other vessels' captains coming aboard the flagship all at once to talk to an admiral'.

Someone standing nearby also decided to drop in on the conversation, uttering:

'Well, if you ask me, it's more than just talk. From the look on the master's face, I'd say it's more of a confrontation, not your occasional cackling', Bartolomé García (the boatswain) suggested, making both Cuéllar and López turn their heads in his voice's direction, after which he proceeded, 'I think they're all onto Colón for some reason… or it could just be de la Cosa finding himself some allies to try to get back at the Admiral for bossing everyone around like he owns it all'.

'You think?', López asked him, putting the plank away.

'Is there something we should be doing about it?', Cuéllar intervened.

García was about to provide them his opinion when yet another voice made itself heard a few feet away:

'Hey! What goes on there? Haven't you business to go about? Save the chatter for your own time. Fall out!'.

It was Diego de Arana, the one man Columbus trusted more than himself to be his eyes on deck in the quality of master-at-arms (obviously overruling de la Cosa's thoughts regarding the matter), reporting back to him should there be talks of divergence among the crew from the Admiral's instructions; even though there was not much space on any of the vessels for that many men to keep a certain distance from each other, which was not particularly safe as far as communal health was concerned, as we have pointed out before, Arana made sure he covered most of the ship's area so that her sailors did not have much time to share their concerns with each other. According to Columbus's point of view, concealment of information was the best tool to keep anyone with an objectional spirit in line, which is probably why he was rendered nearly speechless when Yáñez Pinzón saw right through him, but since Arana had no authority over him, there really was no literal way to stop him, let alone his mind – one of the few things in the world nobody can take control of, no matter how hard they try.

The Santa María's boatswain, carpenter, and joiner promptly followed the master-at-arms' instruction and dispersed, chorally replying:

'Aye, sir'.

Once Arana walked away, García uttered a humorous retort on the former's back, maybe even loud enough for him to hear the wit himself:

'And this, gents, is the Admiral's solution to keep us in our place – a vintner fermenting our juices into liking him! We're three sheets to the wind, sir! Thank you very much!'.

Most of the sailors nearby could not help but chuckle at the sound of the boatswain's remark, which, in a way, could not be further away from the truth, for Arana was indeed a winemaker dwelling in that Córdoba apothecary sponsored by Columbus, so, most naturally, making him an overseer of sailors instead of grape vines did not necessarily command a great deal of respect, something he knew only too well, for which reason he thought it best to just ignore the provocation and go on about his business somewhere else, whispering to himself in a rather melancholic tone:

'Hmm… "in vino veritas"…? More like "in vino vanitas"… bloody seadogs – to hell with all of you'.

***

'Oh!, never mind the damned pleasantries, boy!', de la Cosa interjected toward Pedro de Salcedo, adding, 'Colón may be royalty to you, but this is still my ship and I don't need permission to enter wherever the hell the wind takes me!'.

And just like that, the shipmaster opened the cabin door to find Columbus and Yáñez Pinzón holding each other's forearms in agreement, just as ancient Roman practice had taught them (even though the «chain of command» question was rather unclear).

'What's all this, then…?', de la Cosa inquired, considerably surprised by the fact the Captain of the Niña did not seem nearly as upset as he had been only a few moments before.

'Vicente? What's going on?', Alonso Pinzón asked his brother, entering the cabin ahead of de la Cosa, who, in turn, felt offended for being left behind yet again; still, he was smart enough to withdraw himself from uttering any further complaints, for his archenemy was the one being set afire, and he could perfectly make do with that pleasure alone for the time being.

'How do you mean? Everything's fine', Yáñez Pinzón replied, letting go of Columbus's forearm, a gesture the latter mirrored simultaneously, addressing Alonso Pinzón soon after:

'To what do I owe the pleasure, Captain? I wasn't told you were coming aboard... did you know about this, de la Cosa?', he asked the shipmaster, his tone exceedingly superior.

'Who do you think you're talking to, Colón?! I'm shipmaster, not ship boy, let alone your personal servant!', de la Cosa stressed in an outburst, entering the cabin and slamming the door behind him shut, preventing several pairs of eyes and ears from prying into officer's affairs; Pedro de Salcedo still raised his right hand's index finger as he tried to manage the entrances into the Admiral's cabin, but no one inside seemed to care about etiquette at that time – not even Columbus.

'I'm sorry to interrupt everybody's aching pride', Alonso Pinzón ironically pointed out, 'but I'd like to know what it was my brother came here to tell the Admiral. We can leave the measuring of your manhood for later, thank you very much – preferably after I walk out'.

There were only grown men in that cabin, but neither Columbus nor de la Cosa could help ogling the floorboards with a touch of embarrassment

Columbia: Part I

flowing down their spine. Choosing to put an end to the apparatus before things got any weirder, Yáñez Pinzón came clean:

'Look, Martín... in all honesty, I came here to tell Colón I was going to turn around and head back for Andalusia, given his... miscalculations regarding his initially projected distance, which eventually led to the depletion of our resources; however...', the Captain of the Niña began to explain, until he was interrupted by his brother:

'Well, it's no wonder they're depleted. We've traveled approximately one thousand leagues since we left the Canaries, having only packed enough for no more than eight hundred. Yes, I did the math, Colón... I know how far we've come, even though I can't possibly know where exactly – and neither can you', Alonso Pinzón remarked after realizing how surprised Columbus was, adding, 'I'm sure Vicente made you bear that same look on your face the moment he unraveled your little scheme. I'm also guessing he felt insulted by it, as do I right now. You were the one asking for the best at Palos... did you really think your fellow Captains wouldn't be able to figure out the numbers on their own? We've been sailing for years, and with the easterlies we've had over the course of more than a month, there's absolutely no way we'd be under seven hundred and fifty leagues'.

'You know about the easterlies? Well, I have

underestimated you both, indeed', Columbus said without even thinking of how those words would probably sound to the brothers' ears.

'Oh!, glad I could be of help!', Alonso Pinzón snidely remarked; it was then Columbus realized he had lost too good an opportunity to keep quiet.

Yáñez Pinzón was next to intervene:

'Yes, Colón, we know about the easterlies, just as much as about the westerlies; the Portuguese have taught as well, and that is the path I was planning on taking on the leg back. However, Martín, hear me out – the Admiral here has made me realize we'll probably exhaust the little food and drink we've got if we come about now. This mist that's been sliding over the water has got to be heading somewhere nearby, even if it's no more than a few isles. I've agreed to stay a couple more days until we find them. From there to Cipango... it's probably a few days more, we restock, ask the locals how far to Catayo and that's that. What do you say?'.

Alonso Pinzón paused for a while, left ever-so dumbstruck by his brother's too quick a change of heart. He even blinked uncontrollably, eventually driving his hands all the way up to the height of his face, stammering:

'I... what do I say?', he scoffed, 'I've... I've literally... no idea... at all... whatsoever'.

'You do agree it's a reasonable request, don't you, Pinzón?', Columbus calmly asked him, after

Columbia: Part I

which he noted, 'I mean… westerlies or not, we're going to end up all dead in the middle of the Ocean Sea if we turn back now, so… why not heed your brother's calling? Look, I didn't order him to keep moving, I asked him to stay by my side, and now we both implore you to see reason. We push on, overcome this beginner's disorientation, the trade route is set, your name we'll be forever remembered. After that, do what you will – stay, leave… your decision entirely'.

Alonso Pinzón, who had sat down in the meantime, took a deep breath, looked both Columbus and his brother in their eyes, exerted a chewing motion for a while, and finally spoke, simultaneously raising his right index finger as a sign of both warning and reprimand:

'You should've come to me first before deciding to confront Colón all by yourself', he began to say, pointing to Yáñez Pinzón, adding, 'our whole lives we've spent together, so far, and it's precisely when they're hanging in the balance you choose to act on your own. I must admit the Admiral has a way with words and… yes, I'm also willing to admit the odds of going back now don't look good… we've spent so long at sea that I'm feeling like a landlubber myself, but we could've presented a stronger front together, come up with something else, but… what good would it do us?', he asked, pausing again before turning both his sight and his index to Columbus, to whom he said, 'I'm staying too, but mark my words – I'm not happy you deliberately kept the actual numbers from me, nor am I content with what the men have been going through, so don't think I'm excusing you. I just don't want their demise on my conscience, even though it's far too likely the vermin they're eating now will start chewing on their insides. Also… there's the money I put in on this as well, so…'.

Columbus looked up and raised his arms to the ceiling presently sheltering the four officers in relief, though he was actually reaching for the heavens, saying grace out loud, accompanied by nervous laughter:

'Praise be to God! Ha! That's the spirit, Pinzón, that's the spirit!'.

The outburst was so ominous that it became contagious, spreading like wildfire from the Admiral to the brothers; it was one of those situations in which awkwardness thrives for some reason and the only right thing to do seems to be to play along, so as not to feel embarrassed, and not for oneself, but for the others.

Juan de la Cosa, on the other hand, was not at all buying it, shimmying his sight sideways, leaping from the Captain of the Niña, to the Admiral, to the Captain of the Pinta, and all the way back, repeatedly. If up until then tripartite ridiculousness looked like it was ruling over the scene, it was when the Santa María's shipmaster screamed in anger and frustration that the zenith of whatever was going on in that cabin was achieved:

'You sons of biscuit eaters! Have your minds been twisted and warped by the sirens in these depths?! Only a few minutes ago the both of you were willing to manacle this mercenary all the way back to Spain, and now you're on his side?! How thick can you be to let yourselves be swayed so easily? I see… I get it, it's all become quite clear to me now… this was no more than a ruse! The three of you wanted to purge me all along from this suicidal venture! You're so desperate for gold and spices you don't care how many lives you reap to get them! Well, gentlemen, not anymore! This game is at an end!'.

Rendering Columbus and the Pinzón brothers flabbergasted and dumbstruck, de la Cosa stomped out of the cabin that was his by right, slammed the door and, having quickly produced a keyring from his pocket, wielded a relatively large brass key (the only one found in the ring) and drove it into the old lock, thus ensnaring the top three officers in charge of the enterprise in a confined space whose only way out was also the only way in.

It is rather likely nearly every sailor from the entire flotilla had their eyes glued to de la Cosa, who turned around to face them with a strongly labored breathing. In the quality of both Captain and shipmaster, having relieved the three amigos of their command, he was the one running the operation now, and he certainly was not about to give up his fulfilled lust for power so easily, confident he would find all the support he could get from his crewmembers spread across all three vessels.

Chapter III
The Tables Have Turned

'All right, you lot – listen up! All hands hoay!', Juan de la Cosa cried from the poop deck of La Gallega, his hands resting on the inner taffrail and his voice echoing through the breeze like ripples on the Ocean Sea surface.

Underneath those exact same boards he was standing on like a king, Columbus and the Pinzón brothers were banging on the cabin door with their fists, demanding that the shipmaster release them immediately under penalty of being charged with treason, but their words were barely noticeable, given their current cloistered status. Only de la Cosa could listen a bit clearer because of the crack in the poop deck's floor, but his drive eventually tuned all the ruckus out, proceeding accordingly:

'We've been hornswoggled, comrades! Colón, Yáñez Pinzón, Alonso Pinzón, they've all tricked us into coming to no man's waters without having any idea what they were doing or where they were going! The self-proclaimed Admiral swore to our Queen this journey would take no more than seven hundred and fifty leagues, bringing the Spanish people nothing but prosperity and riches, overcoming Portugal in the control for new silk routes across the Ocean Sea, making our country the most powerful of all nations in the world, with a vaster empire nobody could ever imagine! Well...! Let me say unto you – we are by now a thousand leagues in and both land and booty have yet to be spotted!'.

Whereas a small portion of the flotilla's sailors was rendered speechless for fear of dying out at sea for no justifiable reason, the majority began indistinctly protesting, their rage fueling both the yelling and the will to execute Columbus and the Pinzón brothers by quartering them to bits, only then throwing them into the Ocean Sea as bait.

Disturbed as he had gotten for having been made fun of earlier by the seamen, Diego de Arana realized de la Cosa was apparently taking over only after the latter was already halfway into his speech, also noticing neither Columbus nor the Pinzóns were anywhere in sight, a realization of fact that inevitably made him fear for his life. De la Cosa then continued:

'I have, therefore, come to an important decision that may still save our lives, should we be so lucky! As the master and commander of this flotilla's flagship, I am ordering you all to avast, come about and drop sail, all ahead full! We're going home at last; may God have mercy on our souls… heave ho!'.

Cheering immediately erupted from La Gallega, the Niña, and the Pinta, for the majority of sailors had heard exactly what they had been wanting to hear almost since the very beginning of the journey; a few others could not help but grow exponentially suspicious, considering de la Cosa had constantly been overruled by Columbus throughout the entire journey, but, then again, the Admiral was being accused of driving them all to certain death, and given both Yáñez and Alonso Pinzón had kept following him, never publicly complaining about his ironfisted ruling, the seamen from all three ships figured the Santa María's master was finally standing up for himself, if not the crew entirely, when the so-called "officers" would not.

The word was swiftly spread to the pilots and the flotilla turned their rudders hard-a-port nearly at the same time while the sails were dropped to their full extent, everyone hoping to make it back before it was too late – except, of course, for a few, such as Diego de Arana yet again, whose loyalties lay with Columbus, who, together with the Pinzón brothers, was trapped in the cabin as if it were a brig, soon realizing the whole apparatus was just about to enter a new stage of developments.

There was also Juan Niño, master and owner of the Niña (hence her nickname), who was great friends with the Pinzóns, having even convinced some of the men of Moguer to take part in the enterprise because of the respectability the Pinzón family name commanded when it came to maritime affairs, but he too felt like giving up was probably the best option. His relationship with both Vicente Yáñez and Martín Alonso would probably be left scarred for his inaction, but, in the end, and by agreeing to turn around as per de la Cosa's decision, Juan Niño considered they would eventually thank him for the gut he had mustered, resulting in their safe return home. Not just that, Pedro Alonso Niño, his brother, was a crewman aboard the Santa María – her pilot, to be precise, for which reason the Niña's proprietor did not feel like endangering his own kin by refusing de la Cosa's instructions.

As far as the Pinta was concerned, without Martín Alonso on deck, both Cristóbal Quintero and Gómez Rascón, who Columbus suspected had deliberately damaged their own ship to avoid her

Columbia: Part I

partaking in the trip, may we recall, took over the vessel once again for themselves and were beyond relieved to side with de la Cosa.

In short, the leaders of the voyage had a full plate on their hands to deal with, and it most certainly was not going to be an easy feat to regain control.

***

'What in blazes is happening?! The damned scallywag is turning around! Hey! De la Cosa! I'll have your head for treason, you short-witted privateer! I know you can hear me, maledetto! Open the door this instant! That's an order! Ti strozzo!', the Admiral shouted at the ceiling, where he had just heard a man's footsteps – most likely de la Cosa's, he reckoned; given the situation Yáñez and Alonso Pinzón were in as well, they sided with Columbus a great deal more than up until then, after a whole month in the Canary Islands and another at sea, trying their best to get the attention of anyone at all who could set them free by banging wherever they could, whether it be against the ceiling or the wall facing the quarterdeck.

It was only after a while, when the ships had nearly come about in full, that Columbus banged both his fists against the cabin door, leaning his head against it with his eyes shut, just swallowing hard and hoping some brilliant idea would inflate him into taking an effective course of action; because said hypothetical accomplishment did not strike him, he chose to do that to something else with thunderous wrath – the Admiral went to his desk, shoved all his instruments from the top, subconsciously took hold of his quadrant and threw it against the thick glass of the portside window, where the instrument held in place, marking it with a crack made on a vertical axis. The brass object was the sturdiest item he had been able to find in his quarters. Columbus's impulse eventually caught Yáñez and Alonso Pinzón's attention, for the Pinta, though disfigured, could be seen sailing nearby, leading them to utter the magical word simultaneously:

'Francisco...!'.

The Genoese turned to them as if both had spoken gibberish, unable to process what they meant, deranged as he was, not only because of de la Cosa's betrayal in plain sight, but also because, so it seemed, no one else had even tried to revert the situation they were in – not the masters, not the owners, nobody. He then had to ask, somewhat impatiently and sharply:

'What?!'.

'Our brother, Colón!', Alonso Pinzón replied.

'Francisco Martín!', Yáñez Pinzón further explained.

Columbia: Part I

'There's another one of you traveling with us…?', Columbus asked, complementing his question with an observation the brothers were too excited to get mad at, 'I had no idea, honest to God…!'.

'He's the master of the Pinta, Colón! He spent last night puking, couldn't grab a single wink, let alone forty… sleep must have caught up with him by now, so he's probably out for the count and didn't even notice what's going on… still, I hope neither Quintero nor Rascón got to him', Alonso Pinzón lamented.

'Which is why we need to at least try to find a way to get to him', Yáñez Pinzón reiterated, 'and that there might just be the solution we've been looking for', he added, completing his argument and pointing to the quadrant lodged in the window pane.

The Admiral then realized what it was the brothers were trying to say, uttering the conclusion himself:

'We need to make ourselves heard', a statement to which Yáñez and Alonso Pinzón both nodded in agreement, followed by a teeny snag, 'on both sides'.

Neither Yáñez nor Alonso Pinzón quite understood what Columbus had meant by that, so he explained it to them in a gentle whisper, assuming Juan de la Cosa was still walking all over them, and not just figuratively:

'I need you to be loud while I break the rest of the window and see if I can get Salcedo's attention. With a wee bit of luck, he might have just stayed behind; the problem is the poor lad doesn't know what to do, now. I have to get to him. Whenever you're ready...!'.

The brothers promptly followed the directive and left the Admiral to his personal efforts; Martín Alonso kept hitting the cabin door, while Vicente Yáñez took hold of Columbus's chair, climbed atop his desk, and started banging the roofing, not to mention they were both crying out. Instead of feeling annoyed by the provocation, Juan de la Cosa was actually delighted by the desperation with which the three men were trying to escape, yelling down at the crack in the poop deck:

'You just keep going! Avast ye not! Ha-ha! Scream your lungs out, for all I care! Sooner or later you won't have the strength to keep up! You'll be bait in the water long before we berth where we never should have left from!'.

In between the exchange of black spots, Columbus pickaxed the window as hard as he could, eventually breaking the glass, whose remnants fell into the water, faintly mirroring the Sun's early morning luminosity – a case of cause and effect that, fortunately for the three ensnared men, did draw the attention of the always loyal servant,

Columbia: Part I

Pedro de Salcedo, who had sought refuge down in the orlop, where, up until then, he had kept pacing fore and aft, noticing the phenomenon once he approached the tiller, manned by Pedro Alonso Niño, rendered somewhat intrigued by the ship's boy behavior:

'What? Have you spotted a whale, or something?', the man asked Salcedo, turning back to peek through the gap looking to the sea.

'Erm… no. No – not at all', the boy replied, breaking from the trance, adding, 'I just thought… no, that was probably nothing. Sorry for troubling you, I have to go', he concluded, climbing the stairs to the upper deck while leaving the pilot to shrug his shoulders to himself.

It could have easily been a completely normal event where the surface of the Ocean Sea also reflects light, but the raining of shards out the cabin window, together with a little blood spill from the Admiral's somewhat slashed hands tainting the water, made it clearer for the ship's boy, who had indeed been rendered helpless the moment de la Cosa locked the door. His best chance at finding someone willing to help lay with Diego de Arana, the master-at-arms, but he was being kept under close watch by the same men who did not have a shred of respect for him, in league with the foreigner made more important than any national, and by the Queen herself, no less. No, this called for a distraction – one Columbus looked to bring Salcedo into, hoping the latter would not have gone too far:

'Salcedo!', the Admiral gently called out the window in a whisper, 'Are you there?! I need you, lad!'.

Columbus's personal servant was just arriving to the quarterdeck from the midships section in a hurry, his gaze eventually meeting the Admiral's, who was trying his best to be seen, somehow. In order to better understand what he was saying, Salcedo had to lean outward from the stairs leading up to the poop deck, where Juan de la Cosa was stationed at the moment, his back turned on the ship.

Both Yáñez and Alonso Pinzón were resting from the chaos they had provoked in the cabin while covering for the Admiral, which made the Santa María's master turn around, look down on the floor and ask them:

'Had enough now, have we? Good! That'll teach you not to pick a brawl with me, you dirty seadogs! What…', he began to say, but the sight of Salcedo ogling the side of the vessel like a carpenter assessing damage rendered him intrigued enough to pause and address the boy like so, 'Salcedo! What are you doing? Was it something you saw?'.

The servant nearly slipped overboard when prompted by the shipmaster, but he eventually managed to recover his balance inward. Even though he still had not made clear contact with Columbus, Salcedo knew he had to prevent de la Cosa from peeking down the vessel's portside, otherwise the Admiral's head could easily be spotted trying to reach out.

'No, sir! I... the steps are wet and I almost fell, but... it's all right, now', Salcedo told the shipmaster, climbing the rest of the stairs and swiftly placing himself between the man and the taffrail installed on the poop deck.

Given de la Cosa had just been addressing Columbus and the Pinzón brothers through the floor, the ship's boy figured there must have been a way the master could make himself heard into the cabin, a hypothesis he took into account the next time he spoke, increasing the volume of his voice, but only after de la Cosa posed a question with a squinting expression on his face, as if he were already growing suspicious as to why Salcedo was in the quarterdeck to boot:

'Then what are you doing here? I don't remember telling you to bring me anything... or was it someone else you were trying to reach?'.

Salcedo swallowed hard, fixating his wide-open gaze on de la Cosa's half-shut eyes; if he carried it on any longer, then the shipmaster would definitely want to take a look below, eventually spotting blood stains. The boy simply got into character and told de la Cosa, in a navy-like fashion:

'No, sir! I'm here reporting for duty, sir! Mayordomo Gutiérrez ordered Pedro de Terreros to find me and fetch the ship's Captain, and that is what I've come to do – he requires your presence in the forecastle at once, sir!'.

De la Cosa, though somewhat impressed by the lad's apparent dedication, was not entirely convinced, his squinting much softer and his chin pointing forward, looking rather inquisitive:

'The royal steward wishes to see the Captain, is that right? And was it me he meant? Not, say... Colón?'.

'Absolutely not, sir. The Mayordomo is well aware the former Admiral is incapacitated and now desires to speak to the real commander of this vessel, not someone whose judgment has been compromised', Salcedo explained, lying through his teeth quite audibly.

'Very well. I like this new you, Salcedo – very much so', de la Cosa replied with a grin on his face, picturing the boy's loyalties lay with the strong and victorious, instead of a random person's mere character; he was going down the stairs when, suddenly, he stopped, turning back to he boy to ask him, 'Well...?'.

'Sir?'.

'I should think you'd want to escort me, lad. If

Columbia: Part I

I'm not up here, then what are you staying for? Come along, now. I've business to attend to'.

Salcedo nearly hesitated once more, but sighting the other young man he had involved in his ploy on deck, Terreros, the cabin's boy, Columbus' servant felt relief flowing down his spine once more, reassuring de la Cosa:

'Aye, sir! Not to worry, I will follow you, but Terreros is the one who is going to be taking you inside the officers' quarters, as he is already aware of the matters the Mayordomo desires to speak to you about. I'm afraid my knowledge beyond that door is out of bounds and, therefore, have no business going inside. Besides, the pilot's asked for me'.

De la Cosa was yet again looking for another soft spot to poke in Salcedo's statements, but the boy's nerve took the best of him and he called out to the midships for his counterpart, disabling the inflated owner of the Santa María:

'Terreros! Up here! The Captain is ready for you, now!'.

Needless to say Salcedo caught the cabin's boy by surprise, as he was obviously unaware of any orders whatsoever to bring de la Cosa to the presence of Pedro de Gutiérrez, lodged in the forecastle and most likely unaware a mutiny had taken place. The flotilla really did not comprise vessels so outstanding in size that part of the passengers could afford to miss key moments to the like of coming about or facing a coup (and a loud one, at that) based on personal pride alone, but the place each person took on board had such unclear boundaries that no one really felt at liberty to go either here or there without asking themselves if they should – unless they were sailors, of course, for those had specific instructions to follow on a rotational basis, which, in short, consisted of watchkeeping, trimming the sails to avoid an excessive downwind run, or doing the exact opposite by beating and, consecutively, tacking an upwind, as it is impossible to keep sailing forward with a centered tiller if the wind is blowing straight against the vessel; then again, furling might be required after all if the pressure is overwhelming, instead of exclusively relying on the rudder, as it will only slow down the vessel. Either way, these few examples only prove the deck is meant for seamen, not officials standing post on behalf of the Crown. What was important now was that Pedro de Terreros embark on Pedro de Salcedo's attempt to fool Juan de la Cosa, so the ship's boy could get to his real master as quickly as possible.

'What's that, then?', Terreros asked Salcedo, the look on his face clearly stating he had no idea what all the fuss was about.

'The Captain is ready for you to take him to Mayordomo Gutiérrez, as solicited', Salcedo replied in a firm tone, simultaneously arching his brows and nearly bulging his eyes out of their sockets as to imply the cabin's boy should just move along and take de la Cosa with him, no questions asked – until the shipmaster turned to face Salcedo again, that is, making the latter quickly relax his facial muscles to absolute easement; using his peripheral vision instead of looking directly at de la Cosa would have made it all a great deal more believable, not only to the shipmaster, but the cabin's boy as well, or so he hoped.

'Aye… of course! My apologies, sir. Please follow me – the Mayordomo awaits you', Terreros told de la Cosa, extending his arm as to show the shipmaster the way.

De la Cosa briefly ignored the cabin's boy to look inside Salcedo's eyes, now meeting his own without a single blink. Unable to find any evidence he was being made a fool of, he walked in front of Terreros.

'Aye. Come, boy', he uttered, taking hold of his keyring and jiggling it loud enough for Salcedo to realize there was no opening the cabin door while he was away from the poop deck.

Pedro de Terreros waited for de la Cosa to finally face forward, ogling Salcedo in silence as he shrugged his shoulders and muttered:

'What are you doing…?!'.

'Just trust me…!', the ship's boy vehemently mouthed with that bulgy expression all over his face again.

As de la Cosa and Terreros transversally crossed the midships section, so did Salcedo approach the stairs leading to the orlop, preparing to make his way down to join Pedro Alonso Niño, should the shipmaster surprise him with a sudden peek over his shoulder. However, and given he had the only key to the cabin in his possession, de la Cosa was pretty sure Salcedo would not act against him. Another sight that reassured him of his success in taking over was when his gaze met Diego de Arana's. The master-at-arms, who happened to be unarmed, was being surveilled by García, Cuéllar, and a couple more men; he was defenseless and afraid, which made the shipmaster smile with joy.

Like before, when he had brought Alonso Pinzón aboard to confront Columbus and Yáñez Pinzón in the cabin, de la Cosa approached the forecastle's door and opened it straight away without knocking first, ordering Terreros to follow him in and shut the door behind him. At the center of the room, a small table was in place, and sitting at it were the Mayordomo, Pedro de Gutiérrez, the physician, Juan Sánchez, the Secretary of the Fleet, Rodrigo de Escobedo, and the interpreter, Luis de Torres – they were playing cards; a few others were sound asleep, lying on the thickest pieces of cloth they had found, snoring on their backs. Three of the players moved their head slightly to face de la

Columbia: Part I

Cosa; the doctor, whose back was turned, had to move a tad more, though he was careful enough to conceal his hand from his comrades. His visual acuity adapted to the morning light a few seconds later, Juan Sánchez said:

'Ah!, Master de la Cosa… what a pleasant surprise…! Care to join us for a game of hocca? We're taking lands yet to be found as antes, but the buy-ins go on the table'.

De la Cosa then turned to Terreros with a stern expression, to which the cabin's boy responded with a smile transpiring nothing but constraint.

Chapter IV
Amphibious Assault

'Almirante! Almirante! It is I, Salcedo!'.

Columbus's personal servant had finally pushed through all the obstacles that had been lain between him and his master, having adopted a prone position on top of the poop deck's floor in order to avoid being seen from other spots on the vessel where someone might attempt to stop him. From there, the boy could at last see the Admiral's face, though just partially; it was being able to hear him properly that was important, anyway.

'I saw blood dripping onto the surface... are you and the Captains all right?', the boy asked, worried they might be severely injured.

The three men were already bursting with joy

when Columbus said:

'Pedro, my boy! Thank heavens you're there! We're fine, the three of us are fine! Listen – is de la Cosa nearby...?'.

'No, sir! I came up with an excuse to make him go away, but I'm not sure it'll hold him back much longer... what can I do to help?'.

Yáñez Pinzón then joined the Admiral by the window and gave Salcedo a couple of instructions:

'Salcedo, listen carefully – we need you to find our brother, Francisco. He's the master of the Pinta. He's probably fast asleep and won't have noticed we turned around. Get to him and tell him what happened. He'll know how to handle it from there'.

'But sir, how do I reach him...? If I call him out, Señor de la Cosa will throw me overboard!'.

'Can you get Diego to assist you?', Columbus asked.

'No, sir... I'm afraid the master-at-arms is somewhat helpless at the moment...', Salcedo lamented.

'Is he all right?! Did someone hurt him?!'.

'He's safe, Admiral, don't worry...! It's just that some of the men are in charge of keeping an eye on him like hawks'.

'That scoundrel! Believe me, Pinzón, I'll have his head before nightfall – you mark my words!', Columbus exasperated toward Vicente Yáñez.

Columbia: Part I

Having no other choice, Martín Alonso intervened and spoke directly to Salcedo, the three ensnared men nearly joining their faces by the window:

'There's another way, Salcedo, but you're going to have to be brave incredibly brave – the lives of about ninety men lay on your shoulders, including your own'.

'I'll do whatever it takes, Captain. Just give me the order', the ship's boy replied.

'Do you see the rowboat tugged by the stern of the Pinta? You have to get to it, find your way up the towline and reach the orlop. Francisco will be there', Alonso Pinzón explained.

Rendered confused by the suggestion, Salcedo just had to ask:

'But sir, how am I supposed to reach the rowboat…?'.

'I think you know, lad – jump in the water and swim as fast as you can before the wind pulls us away and you turn into fish fodder', the Captain of the Pinta responded.

'Cosa…? Was that your plan all along? Risking the life of my servant?', Columbus retorted, unhappy about Alonso Pinzón's intentions, adding still, 'All he needs to do is take hold of the key and set us free!'.

'Let's say he does, Colón. What then? They can easily make us walk the plank and finish it once and for all. It's useless without firearms. Even if we had our blades with us, we'd be outnumbered', Alonso Pinzón remarked.

'Would you rather jump out the window yourself?', Yáñez Pinzón ironically suggested.

The Admiral wanted to say no, of course, but he also did not wish to look like a coward in front of the men he still deemed to be his subordinates deep inside. His expression transpired more than he thought, but he believed Salcedo had rescued him just in time once he said:

'Qué pues! No, Captain, the Admiral won't be jumping anywhere. I owe him my life, so if I die for him, I'll have fulfilled my duty, but not until I find Master Pinzón and bring back all the harquebuses I can'.

Climbing atop the taffrail would have likely resulted in someone spotting the boy, whether it be from La Gallega or one of the other two vessels, for which reason Salcedo chose to turn around while lying down so he could then hang from the ship and look better inside the cabin. Columbus took a firm hold of his forearm and, with his voice breaking and a faint smile, said:

'Godspeed, son. We'll be waiting for you'.

Salcedo graciously nodded. Then, he turned back to make sure he was well aware of the rowboat's position in the water. It was only a few feet away and still behind La Gallega, though it would

Columbia: Part I

not take the Pinta much longer to move on ahead and take any chance at success away.

Having taken a deep breath, Salcedo jumped into the Ocean Sea, praying to Almighty God no depth-lurking creature attacked him, foundering his only hope. Fortunately for the men involved, the splash was faint. The boy knew not what to expect the moment he hit the water, but he had figured the temperature would not be the most pleasant; it turns out he was wrong – he simply had never felt the sea offer him that much warmth. Apparently, the currents in that location were the entire opposite of what everyone else was used to back in Europe; perhaps the same went on down the African coast, but he had never been there, so he could not be sure. Only a couple of seconds later, Salcedo rose back to the surface and, focusing on the Pinta's rowboat, drew the wet hair away from his eyes and swam as fast as he could without ever looking back. From above, Columbus and the Pinzón brothers silently cheered him on. He eventually made it – though he had some trouble at first keeping the boat from capsizing because of his weight, made heavier due to his soaked clothing, he spun on himself and fell in, landing on his back.

All he needed now, as his heart decelerated, was to find a way in while remaining unnoticed. As he examined the Pinta's stern, looking for anyone who might have seen him (though no one had), he also realized his youthful physiognomy may just be appropriate enough to squeeze through the gap across which the tiller was maneuvered, as there was a relatively open space immediately above for the pilot to look out and make sure the rudder was functional. Inhaling and exhaling in order to reacquire the necessary nerve, he spun yet again on himself and stood up, ready to take hold of the line and make his way up. The way it felt so damp between his hands made Salcedo think he would end up losing his grip, and the tighter he held, the more difficult it seemed to hold on, but the truth is he made it to the rudder, having to do a bit of contortionism to hang in there and avoid slipping at all costs. With a bit more effort, he was able to align himself with the space above and look inside the ship. The pilot was doing his job, manning his station; he seemed to be alone. No one was providing him any guidelines at the moment. Alonso Pinzón would normally be the man delivering them, but he was presently inaccessible, as we know. Salcedo would have to take him down, somehow, though violence was not his forte; plus, having a good enough physiognomy to crawl in through the tiller gap meant he was not the strapping kind of fellow. He then looked down to the rowboat yet again and realized he should have brought something with him – namely, an oar.

From the Santa María's cabin window, neither

the Admiral nor the Pinzón brothers realized what on earth the boy was doing, climbing back down. The latter actually thought he had gotten too scared and was planning on releasing the boat, abandoning them to their demise, but Columbus was far more optimistic:

'Please, gentlemen! The boy swore not five minutes ago he'd gladly give up his life for our freedom – out of this damned cabin, that is, not the kind we'd be forced to abandon our mortal coil. Just wait, he must have something on his mind'.

Indeed, Salcedo's return to the rowboat obviously had a legitimate drive, and that was acquiring one of the oars for self-defense.

'There, you see? I told you he wasn't going to row away', Columbus stressed.

The oar, however, was not necessarily easy to wield, given its length. Tearing it in half was also out of the question – its thickness was deliberate, otherwise it could easily break when used for its original paddling purpose. Still, the ship's boy sought to tug it between his legs, thus freeing his hands to take hold of the line, constituting a problem of its own, nevertheless, as tightening his joints together too much also increased friction, especially around the knee and ankle areas. As agile as he might have been on account of the little time he had spent on this earthly plane so far, the whole apparatus was not at all an easy feat.

'Ándale, Salcedo…! don't give up on us now…', Alonso Pinzón murmured.

The boy had no intention of doing so. It took him a little longer to climb the towline back up again, but he had made it, seeking to get as close as possible to the surface of the rudder. As far as the next maneuver was concerned, it required a great deal of both balance and concentration, for Salcedo had to jump for the rudder while holding the oar with only one hand, thus freeing the other. It was a risky stunt, naturally, and not just because of the acrobatics, but also due to the constant clashing of the waves against the rudder, no matter how low their cresting – the splashing took care of reaching the higher ground, so to speak. Yet another variable was the noise grabbing the outer end of the tiller would make – once the sound was produced, Salcedo would have to be ready to do something about the pilot. It was now or never. Crouching atop the towline, the oar in his right hand positioned like a spear and his left grabbing on to avoid falling, the lad closed his eyes, took a deep breath, opened his eyes again and went for it. Counting on a leap of faith alone, Salcedo was able to hold on to the surface of the tiller, his hand slipping soon after. Fear not, however, for God was not yet done with him to make him fall and perish by either drowning or full blood loss caused by the attacks of unknown sea creatures every mariner in his right mind feared above anything else when sailing (except for rock formations, maybe, as had been the case with the Cape of Good Hope, dubbed the «Cape of Storms» long before Bartolomeu Dias's heroic feat); no, the Creator still had plans for the boy, which is why he was still able to hold on to the ship's keel, where the rudder had been installed based on a pintle and gudgeon system. That particular area was not affected by the tiller when turning, so Salcedo was relatively safe; it was the sound of the oar's tip hitting the stern due to the rebound of the boy's slip that alerted the pilot to an unusual noise. The rudder had been sabotaged before, so it was likely its repairing during the long stay in the Canaries could have been faulty, taking all that time to show it.

'Aw!, heck…! I just hope we didn't get another hinge broken, otherwise we're done for it – and this time for sure', the Pinta's pilot uttered, tying the tiller handle to two lines, thus centering and blocking it in place.

The pilot began by squeezing through the gap via the ship's portside, failing to notice any damage. He then went back and squeezed once more, this time through the starboard side, where he was surprised by Salcedo hanging by a thread. Startled by the boy, the pilot instinctively retreated upward, instead of just going back due to the limited space, resulting in his hitting the back of his head. The force of the blow quickly brought the pilot excruciating pain, making him close his eyes, take both his hands to the spot in order to assess the presence of blood and massage the throbbing vessels radiating soreness all over. Luckily, he did not scream, but he did hiss profusely through his teeth, almost resembling an asp in sound. Reminding himself he had seen someone hanging from the rudder he had been manning up until then, he reopened his eyes to make sure it had not just been a vision, in which case he would have to do something, such as getting rid of the unwanted presence. The moment his lids began their motion, the last thing the pilot would remember seeing before being knocked out would be the oar's spoon hitting him straight in his forehead, just lying there for a while as if he were as good as dead – so much so the support of his legs naturally gave in to the upper body's weight and the pilot slid back inside, dropping to the floor on his back, hitting the back of his head once more; the pain, of course, would only resonate the moment he came back to his senses. For the time being, he was all right.

As all of these moments went by, the Pinta eventually gained a fair bit of advantage over La Gallega, making it possible for Columbus and the Pinzón brothers to better realize what was happening, reacting both timely and appropriately; for instance, the minute Salcedo made the jump to grab the outer surface of the tiller handle, they gasped in shock, their hearts racing from what could have been a tragedy. As for when the pilot was fed the oar's spoon, they exclaimed in unison:

'Ow...!', laughing in derision, almost forgetting to keep quiet, given the circumstances did not yet allow cheerful manifestations; we must not disregard Salcedo was still figuratively on the balance, though hanging for real.

In order to assist his final climb onto the Pinta's orlop, the boy firmly held the oar's shaft, introduced it through the narrowest spot the tiller handle turned to when moving starboard, and twisted it to render the spoon vertical, thus managing to somewhat secure an anchor point. With a great deal of effort involved, especially after having hung on one hand for so long, Salcedo managed to gain enough momentum to heave himself onto the tiller's surface, resting a while before going in after Francisco Martín Pinzón; as for the pilot, he was still out cold.

'Muy bien, Salcedo! Por Dios, he's done it...! Thank you, Lord!', Columbus exclaimed, joining the palms of his hands and intertwining his fingers in prayer while looking up to the sky through the window; not to presume, but it seemed like the Admiral had developed an idiomatic pattern, fetching his native tongue in times of stress and enrolling in Castilian when celebrating... indeed, it definitely seemed that way.

Columbus and the Pinzón brothers' joy was suddenly interrupted once more when one of the Pinta's co-owners, Gómez Rascón, walked aft and onto the poop deck; Cristóbal Quintero, on the other hand, was in the midships section. The three trapped men crouched almost simultaneously, so as to avoid being seen by yet another who the Admiral deemed to be a traitor. Rascón leaned over the taffrail and looked down, suspecting he had heard some kind of noise, but he eventually found nothing. Salcedo was already inside the vessel, having just finished retracting the oar, which made the co-proprietor miss it by just a thread. Still, and to the boy's horror, Rascón asked a question he knew had to be for the pilot, lying there by his side, rendered unconscious:

'Is everything all right down there?!'.

Salcedo considered replying aloud, but he did not know what the pilot sounded like; a difference in voice register, no matter how small, could be fatal. Gesturing would probably be best, but the boy's arm was not as hairy as the pilot's. This amount of detail was beginning to drive Salcedo beyond crazy; while it is true he had sworn unmistakable loyalty to his master, getting on that rowboat and paddling away could have indeed been a better option, though he would never confess to it if questioned. He had to think fast, or there would be hell to pay, should Rascón head down to the orlop and make sure everything was all right in fact with his own eyes.

The most recognizable gesture demonstrating either a positive answer or outcome was the thumbs-up, passed on as cultural heritage across multiple generations since the Ancient Roman Empire. Considering the pilot was inanimate, how could Salcedo lift his thumb to make it believable? He had to raise it somehow. All the lines in store nearby were too thick to wrap around a finger – except for those of which clothes were made. The boy quickly knelt, held on to one of the folds of the pilot's shirt and pulled, severing it with his teeth once the length became satisfactory. Then, he took the pilot's right hand and turned it into a wrapping, bending his other four fingers while tying a knot to the wrist that would make the thumb stick out. With a little effort, Salcedo grabbed the man under his arms, locked hands at the center of his chest, and leaned him against the tiller handle gap, extending the pilot's arm out as if he were indeed confirming all was fine.

'All right, then! Thought I heard something. Carry on!', Gómez Rascón told the pilot (or so he thought), turning on his feet and walking toward the desk Alonso Pinzón had been working on, making out the actual numbers.

The Pinta's co-owner did not care much for the

Captain's calculations; they were already heading back, and even if they had been close to finding land, he would not have wanted to make it easy for anyone else who decided to better stock his vessel and force him to go through that torment under the provisions of a royal decree a second time, for which reason he tore the charts into smithereens and scattered them in the wind. The roundtrip did not require any special planning; all they had to do (Rascón, Quintero, de la Cosa, and Niño) was keep heading back the way they came, but whether they knew how the cycle pattern the Ocean Sea winds took worked, well… that was something else entirely. Tacking in about twenty-three-degree angles against an upwind was a sharp tactic, but it also took much longer and a great deal more effort from the pilots, who were already exhausted enough as it is after a thousand leagues going straight West, with only a few minor adjustments toward either West-southwest or Southwest in full, let alone constantly diverting toward East-southeast, East, and East-northeast, even – one after the other… they were bound to burst a few blisters, and not just on their hands and feet; also, any sharp turns would eventually end up costing them more precious time, a luxury they could not afford, as the drag created by a rudder almost entirely parallel to the vessel's stern was yet another obstacle to watch out for.

Columbia: Part I

Only one deck above the cargo hold was Pedro de Salcedo, fulfilling his mission to the best of his ability, looking for Francisco Martín Pinzón and, within him, a decisive ally who could help turn the tide – and not just figuratively. Before he could move along any further, however, the pilot required immobilization and, whenever he woke up, whether it be sooner or later, silencing, for which reason Salcedo took it upon himself to grab one of the lines stored next to the tiller and refrain the man from any attempt at moving; as for the distress call he was more than likely to cry out once he realized his arms and legs had been tied together, the boy tore a piece of the pilot's trousers and inserted it in the latter's mouth, effectively gagging him. All that was left regarding this issue was concealing his presence; while it would have probably been much easier to shove him through the tiller handle gap and throw him overboard, murder was out of bounds. The pilot was already defenseless and unaware; getting rid of him so cheaply would only haunt the boy for years to come. It is true a mutiny was taking place, just as much as it was true the rebels would probably end up being punished one way or another, but it was not Salcedo's place to play judge, let alone God, sentencing his companions to their demise without trial. The whole point of this side enterprise (getting things back on track, that is) was to save the lives of ninety men by restoring the Admiral his command of the main venture. Having his rank acknowledged once more, he would have the power to decide what to do with the sailors involved.

And so it was that Salcedo gently pushed the pilot toward the corner, covering him with more lines and a few pulleys, one at a time, thus weighing the man down against the orlop floor.

What lay ahead could only be seen at close range with the aid of a lamp, given the flotilla was sailing against the Sun's position and could not benefit from its luminosity. While the Islamic world was progressively beginning to question Ptolemy's geocentric model of the Universe, the concept that the Earth revolved around the Sun, instead of the other way around, had yet to be proven beyond mere speculation, which is why we can assert the firmament was the one whose movement was required in order for the Sun to cast its light from the West, just moments before merging with the horizon. Waiting for that particular instance, however, would take an entire day and, as explained only a couple of parchment sheets ago, time was of the essence.

Salcedo unhooked the lamp from the Pinta's wooden wall and took hold of it with his left hand, extending his arm and positioning it slightly above his head as far as it would reach, taking the oar with him in his right, for he knew not how many other crewmen lurking in the dark would have to be beaten with a rowing instrument before he reached his target. Since no one had stopped him on his way so far, he wanted to believe no more confrontation would be necessary.

An aft-to-fore inspection of the deck proved unproductive as far as finding people was concerned, but the stench making its way up Salcedo's nose made him think for a moment there were bodies nearby, which was obviously unsanitary; if someone had passed, then they simply had to be thrown overboard. Then again, it is possible no one had yet noticed whoever was lying there lifeless had disappeared. The foul odor was but one stimulus the boy was facing in that moment – squeaking had become clearer the further he moved. Remains of putrefied meat, worm-harboring fruit, moldy bread, and greens whose original color could not be described anymore for lack of visual evidence could be seen spread all over the deck. Barrels once filled with freshwater were now at their lowest level, the only remaining drops presenting with a shade of yellow, likely tainted with urine; whether it was human, Salcedo could not say. He certainly did not feel like tasting just to make sure, but the truth is he felt weak after leering at all the food gone bad; he had not yet eaten throughout the whole morning and noon was probably on its way.

As it turns out, his focus on the success of the task at hand had prevented him from feeling neither hunger nor thirst, but the body craves what it must, and actually looking at both edible and drinkable resources only worsens the need; the problem was nothing he had found so far was in fact edible or drinkable, unless self-poisoning ever crossed his mind, that is. He was having mixed feelings toward the situation, meaning he craved for nutrition while simultaneously feeling nauseated from the smell of what had once been wine, now turned into vinegar; he looked like he was going to be sick, even though there was nothing in his stomach to throw up except for bile, maybe. The oar was both eventually and unintentionally transformed into a makeshift staff to help Salcedo stand on his feet, but it was all becoming too much to bear; still, he felt conscious enough to put the lamp down inside one of the barrels with just enough water (together with whatever it was mixed with) to put the fire out, should it tip over.

Given he was trying to look for something he could ingest without dying just a few hours later, perhaps placing the lamp inside a barrel was ill-advised, as his vision had obviously become a lot more impaired than before; then again, maybe he wanted to find whichever piece of food he could get a hold of without looking at it, or he might just resist nibbling (let alone biting) through it. Feeling his way around, the boy eventually caught something reasonably soft and fleshy behind what felt like a few baskets covered with torn, perforated cloths. The air was too crowded with different smells to make sure what was in his hand could in fact be eaten without any concern for his already poor health and the need to satiate his stomach was becoming greater by the minute, anyway.

Salcedo thus fell on his knees and leaned the oar against the ship's wall, sitting on his heels while he pursed and rested his lips on the piece of meat (so he figured) he was holding; for a moment, it felt like it had moved, but it was likely his weakened mind was merely playing tricks on him. Touching it with his tongue presented with an odd sensation, odder than the possibility of it moving – it felt furry, which means it could have also been a peach, for instance. Before he lost his nerve by overthinking the issue, he meant to just clench his teeth on that improvised meal straight away and chew as fast as he could; the moment he did, the small chunk of food contorted and squealed in agony, suddenly revealing two small, red orbs fixating him. To his unimaginable horror, Salcedo had just bitten a dazed mouse – or rat, judging from its size, though he could not be sure. Truth be told, the last thing he felt sure of before passing out was his guts seeking to abandon his body from his mouth as a series of other pairs of small, red eyes leered at him like a fresh meal whose taste every one of those rodents animalistically craved, as was their nature. If it had not been for an alerting presence waving another lamp to scare the little imps away back into the dark, Salcedo would have definitely played the role of a main course for a family of parasites which, in turn, carried parasites of their own – the kind that spread none other than the Black Death; it had all started aboard twelve ships crammed up with both corpses covered in a «Great Pestilence» and other mariners who were still alive, though hanging by no more than a thread, with pustules growing everywhere on their body, especially the groin and the armpits, oozing pus and blood, accompanied by other symptoms to the likes of fever, vomiting, diarrhea, generalized pain... in short, a complete and utter mess. Having come to an end for the majority of the European population no more than one hundred and fifty years prior to this occasion did not mean it could not happen again, regardless of the by now regular quarantine practice.

***

'Come, lad, wake up... it's all right, now... you're safe. Drink this, it'll make you feel more alive – and comely, by the way', a voice was heard in the distance – or so it seemed, at least.

He who was coming back to his usual self was none other than Pedro de Salcedo. The boy was just waking up after what it felt to him like multiple hours had gone by. He did not know who, but someone was supporting the back of his head in the palm of their hand while insisting that he drink the contents of a wooden cup, which eventually made his throat react to the somewhat invasive gesture, not out of spite, obviously, but because the concoction was immensely strong, whichever it was, and he was only just recovering his bodily faculties.

'Don't spit it out, just take it and swallow. There, you see? They don't call them "strong spirits" for nothing, now, do they?', the mysterious voice uttered again, progressively sounding closer.

Salcedo's visual acuity was still undergoing a natural enhancement stage, but he did perceive the amount of light was scarce and seemingly radiating from one spot alone, uncovering very few spatial references.

'Where… where am I…?', the boy asked his yet unknown company.

'Where no one can find us – in the Pinta's hold. You weren't originally aboard this vessel, were you? Because I don't seem to recall your face. None of my sailors are as young as you…', the voice remarked, adding, 'Wait… aren't you the Admiral's servant? You are, aren't you? Aye, now I remember... you were always around him back in La Gomera while we were fixing the rudder. Quevedo, isn't it?', the voice replied.

'N-No, it's Sal... Salcedo, Pedro de Salcedo', the boy corrected the stranger while gently coughing a bit more, trying to find his face through the sound of his speech, considering the picture was still slightly distorted, asking also, 'What am I drinking...? Is this poison...?'.

'Hah! No, lad! If I wanted to poison you, I'd let you eat that rat and get eaten by the lot of them! You'd die one way or another, that's for sure. I'm giving you mead, and it's from my personal stash, so stop spitting it out. More than rudeness, it's a complete waste. Oh!, and sorry about your name, by the way. Still, it was close enough, wasn't it? So anyway, what are you doing here? And more importantly – how did you come aboard? I thought that pig from the Santa María was now in command and that he certainly wouldn't let you be wandering about after locking Colón and my brothers up... you know, in case you got any ideas'.

After focusing specifically on that last part of the stranger's remarks (which helped him immensely forget about the fact he had almost eaten a rodent), Salcedo literally pulled himself together, blinked several times and finally saw a face taking

Columbia: Part I

shape; then, he asked the ten thousand-maravedi questions:

'Wait… your brothers…? You're Francisco Pinzón…? The shipmaster?!'.

'That's right, Master Salcedo – "aye" to all three questions, the latter of which probably the most shameful, given the current circumstances… a shipmaster hiding amid his own vessel's cargo. Wouldn't you just know it, eh?', Martín Pinzón regrettably murmured.

'But… so you mean to say you know what's happening? Captain Alonso Pinzón said you'd felt sick all night and that you were probably sleeping, unaware of the mutiny', Salcedo explained.

'Oh!, Dios mío…!', the third Pinzón brother interjected, 'I was only a little sick… it's not like I spent the whole night puking. Martín thinks I can't hold down my liquor, but I can…! And I assume that by "sleeping" he meant I was passed out from all the supposed drinking I've had, right? Just because he's the eldest of the three doesn't mean he has better control over himself. You know, you should've seen him this one time back in Palos – he was so tipsy he almost walked over the shards of his own empty bottles barefooted, swear to God! If it hadn't been for me…', Martín Pinzón ranted, until he was stopped by Salcedo.

'Sir? I'm sorry for interrupting you, but I'm not here to judge how much liquor you can or can't hold down without hurling. The truth of the matter is I was sent here under direct orders from the Admiral and your brothers. Captain Alonso Pinzón told me to come to you and ask you for help resetting our course. Master de la Cosa swayed everyone to turn around and the Admiral figures we'll die of thirst and starvation before we return to Andalusia, but there's nothing neither him nor your brothers can do because... they're locked up... in the cabin...', the boy explained, hesitating once he uttered the last few words, realizing Martín Pinzón had already mentioned it.

'What?', the Pinta's master asked him.

'How long have you known your brothers were relieved?!', Salcedo inquired in disbelief.

'Since the early morning, of course. I told you I wasn't out cold! I'll be damned if I ever get a hangover in my life!', Martín Pinzón exclaimed, standing up for his drinking pride; realizing Salcedo's face remained unchanged, the man proceeded, 'Well... never mind that now. The point is I was well awake, about to grab a spot of breakfast from upstairs, when I heard de la Cosa's speech, loud and clear. It's as if he'd conquered the heavens from God Himself, the way his voice came out of him so loud, breaking all sorts of barriers. Still, I didn't want to believe he'd actually gotten rid of Colón, Vicente, and Martín, but I got my confirmation from all the commotion up on deck, so I

Columbia: Part I

decided I'd meet my best chances in hiding, I mean… if the top had already been disabled, it wouldn't take long until these seadogs got to me. I would've started shooting and slaying them if it weren't for a minor detail…', the shipmaster lamented.

'What?!', Salcedo asked him in desperation.

'Ave María, muchacho! What do you think?! I'm outnumbered! One against twenty-four?! Caracoles, what are the odds of that going well?! Do you even know how those harquebuses work? You need to refill them with gunpowder for every shot and light the fuse each time on both ends! It takes forever to reload and there's a huge chance you'll blow your face off if you're not careful. Even if I took several loaded with me all at once, someone would definitely find the time to grab one and shoot me before I was done with the first couple of rounds, or even slice my belly open with a blade and degut me right there on the spot like a fish. Forget it, there's no possible way'.

'Ugh…!', Salcedo exclaimed, realizing how difficult it was for the mission to be successful, asking himself what the whole point of it had been, 'Then what am I doing here?! I've never handled a gun before and I'm definitely not a swordsman… this doesn't make any sense. They're smart men, all three of them – they must've wanted me to do something apart from finding you…'.

Martín Pinzón looked at the boy with a frown, disappointed his high hopes had just vanished into thin air. Still, he tried to make it up to him with somewhat of a jest:

'Well, if you think you can knock most of them out with that oar of yours, we can try to make a run for it and disable as many as we can, but it's still just two against more than twenty...'.

Salcedo exhaled through his nose with a slight twist of the corner of his mouth, showing appreciation for the zinger, but it still did not solve the problem at hand. As he leaned against the wall of the ship's hull, looking into the void, he replayed bits of Martín Pinzón's oratory in his mind, the most important of which gave him an idea, bringing stronger light to his eyes than the wobbly flame inside the lamp:

'Sir...? How many guns and blades have you got down here...?'.

'About five firearms, ten swords... not everyone here is an admirer of both, so they get to pick what they're most comfortable with, though, judging from the numbers, you can tell the majority is old-fashioned. Plus, there are those who don't feel like wielding any sort of weapon whatsoever, so they're not even armed. Come to think of it, nobody is at the moment. There's been resistance to this voyage since the very beginning, so I told Martín it was probably best to just keep them away from the men's sight, but still… they took over all the same. Why do you ask, anyway?', Martín Pinzón inquired, after his reflection on the mariners' different characters.

'That thing you said about the oar, Master… I still haven't told you how I came aboard – I dove into the water and swam to the rowboat tugged behind the vessel. I had nothing to fend myself with, so I took one of the oars with me. That's how I got rid of the pilot – I knocked him out with a blow to the head, but that's irrelevant now. What's important is this: if I manage to get back into the boat and carry a few blades and guns with me, maybe I can get them to the Admiral and the Captains! And if anyone spots and tries to stop me, you can provide cover – just shoot them!'.

Martín Pinzón remained pensive for quite some time, gazing into the boy's sparkling irises.

'Hmm…', he uttered, squinting his own sight in an inquisitive manner until his eyes were rendered shut.

Salcedo stared at him for a while as well, failing to realize what was going through the shipmaster's mind; maybe he was not thinking at all, but rather asleep from all the booze. At least it looked that way, judging from his consistently timely breathing. The boy gradually lost his smile, frowned and crossed his arms over his chest, expressing his disappointment aloud:

'Ah!, venga...! This is whose shoulders hope was lying on all this time – a drunk...!'.

As Salcedo finished his venting, so was Martín Pinzón exhaling every bit of air inside his lungs, only to inhale deeply once more and categorically state, to the boy's surprise:

'I've only just told you, niñito – I can hold down my liquor and I'll be damned if I ever get a hangover!'.

Salcedo swallowed hard, facing him while looking for the shipmaster's eyes of disapproval, though he kept them closed. Instead, he proceeded:

'I'm thinking, that's all. Your proposal makes sense. It's risky, but it's all we've got. I don't feel like sailing into a storm while these imbeciles keep asking each other what they're supposed to do about it. Plus, sooner or later I'll run out of nerve, mead, and bread, and not necessarily in that order. Night hasn't yet fallen. We must wait until dark to better move around. In the meantime, we conjure up a plan. Grabbing swords and guns just like that and hoping they'll do us good on their own because of the quantity won't get us anywhere, except maybe killed – and much faster than fasting. Now, close your eyes, and let's see what comes up. Take a bite and drink some more, too. A man's brains can't function properly if his stomach is starving and his thirst is left unquenched. Don't you worry, boy – we'll come up with something'.

Columbia: Part I

Salcedo had been mistaken after all. The words that came out of Martín Pinzón's mouth were so very much filled with wisdom that the boy did not question his judgment ever again, uttering in an apologetic tone:

'Yes, Master'.

***

'The Sun's nearly gone…', Yáñez Pinzón remarked, looking out in the horizon through the broken cabin window, where the ultimate source of daylight seemed to be progressively merging with the sea, eventually becoming one.

'Indeed', Columbus replied in an unhappy tone mixed with rage, adding, 'an entire day wasted sailing back… to what?! Porca miseria!', he interjected, kicking toward the back of the cabin the bloodstained quadrant that only about twelve hours prior had seemed ever-so promising regarding his and the Pinzón brothers' freedom.

'By now, we can only suppose Salcedo was caught… and it all looked like it was going so well in the beginning…', Alonso Pinzón lamented, his stomach loudly urging him to feed it soon.

Meanwhile, the flotilla, now on its way back and presumed unstoppable under the command of Juan de la Cosa, had progressively become quiet. Sailors working all day long had just yielded their spot to the night shift, who had not slept much during the day, on account of the sudden change of plans following the impromptu seize of power and its high praise from those wide-awake after enjoying a good night's sleep – as far as "good" went aboard three vessels with little privacy and absolutely zero comfort, that is. A great deal of the mariners now taking over were currently struggling to even stand, as opposed to the barrelmen keeping watch from the crow's nests, who did not bother trying to look busy; of the three performing the task at hand, they either leaned against the main mast in an upright position with their eyes shut while sitting down, only to make sure their head was visible, or they simply lay down in a fetal position, as if the structure supporting their weight up above was no more than an adult-sized wooden womb, hoping to nap for as long as possible without getting caught. Even though they were the ones playing the role of lookouts, placed higher than anyone else aboard either vessel, these barrels cut in half sufficiently restricted the airflow, which had been at a pleasant temperature throughout most of the journey, given summer was not yet ready to leave, but now, as autumn made itself at home on the eve of October the eighth, so did its unmistakable nocturnal chills. Still, the winds were calm enough as to refrain from generating all sorts of weatherly hazards – especially typhoons; the fact the flotilla had not yet found itself in the middle of a storm gifted with constant precipitation and strong winds, which would likely be a product of monsoon season, Columbus considered (prior to having to worry about the loss of command), was due to the withdrawal the phenomenon was subjected to by the end of August, according to Marco Polo's observations during his long stay in East Asia, which means the voyage's timing, while tampered with because of Cristóbal Quintero and Gómez Rascón's betrayal, had been far too lucky. Initially, the Admiral had interpreted it as a sign of divine will, urging him to sail away only when it was safe to do so. However, and now that the whole enterprise was literally going the opposite way, Columbus was not so sure God intended for him to see it through, anymore.

Suddenly, however, and after spending most of the day beating the upwind, the sails were furled completely. The flotilla's present location had no wind for the seamen to rely on, and so they had no choice but to stop for the night, though no anchor was dropped, as the depth was still unknown and the uncontrolled release of the lines could easily tear the ships apart; the vessels' positioning could only be, therefore, secured with visual reference from the firmament.

After the first day Juan de la Cosa had finally been show some respect, the first day of glory for most of the crew, eager to sail back home, the shipmaster and reinstated Captain (a rank he had always held as far as he was concerned, despite direct overruling and confrontation from the Admiral) retired to the forecastle, where he intended to rest just for the night, transferring the prisoners from the cabin to the hull first thing in the morning, where they would join the manacled officials of the royal court, including the hocca players from earlier, thus retrieving the cabin for himself and allowing his men to have a ceiling over their heads in their own time, when their shift was over.

Suffice it to say that, the way things looked, neither Queen Isabella nor King Fernando II were being represented aboard the flotilla – not anymore, at least; whether it be the Mayordomo, the Secretary of the Fleet, the doctor, the Lord of the Wardrobes, it did not matter. In short, none of the nobility, the elite, the "Dons", whichever the designation, were in charge. More importantly to de la Cosa, the fake "Don" and Admiral, Columbus, had been the first to be excluded from the chain of command, and that was an undeniable major victory; entrapping the other two captains along with him, more than a lucky streak, had been a bonus he could peacefully relish in his much deserved rest, hoping to smile as he dreamt about mooring in Palos de la Frontera; being homesick was a kind of sickness, after all.

Columbia: Part I

As darkness progressively engulfed the sailing trio, a few lamps were lit on deck, though the light they radiated was weak, solely reliant on the power of the fire within them claimed from the fuel chamber. In the cabin of the Santa María, the oil of the lamp hanging from the ceiling was running out, eventually dimming all luminosity the flame emitted, contorting itself to its figurative knees, as if gasping, yearning for air, until only the stars remained above, in the gyrating celestial dome. Neither Columbus, nor Yáñez Pinzón, nor Alonso Pinzón uttered a word; silence did not feel awkward at present – it was talking to state the obvious that would have made the ordeal worse.

Not too far, to the Santa María's portside, movement was taking place in the Pinta's entrails. Pedro de Salcedo and Francisco Martín Pinzón were finally putting their plan to work. With only one lamp for a guiding source, held in front of the pair by Salcedo, who was also wielding a sharp blade (instead of the blunt oar he had used before) and carrying a few firearms and swords on his back, tied to each other with the help of a severed line taken from a spare pulley, Martín Pinzón had a harquebus ready to fire, its stock held against his right shoulder, the palm of the hand on the same side placed under it, the index bent in front of the trigger, prepared to squeeze it when necessary, and his left hand supporting the barrel, as opposed to the common fork rests, which were being saved for later, also tied to his back, along with a few more guns and at least one extra sword, just in case he had to use both, should the firearms be rendered impractical and ultimately useless.

They were both climbing the staircase leading up to the orlop, where Salcedo had passed out and the tiller was located. The chaffing sound the blades made at each step taken forward was beginning to unnerve the boy, fearing someone might hear them, no matter how faint the noise was. They were, after all, aboard a ship entirely made of wood, which was not the best of resources should one desire to remain silent to third-party ears.

The moment they emerged, Martín Pinzón stopped Salcedo from moving any further by resting his left hand on the boy's right shoulder; the gesture, however, did not scare him into pissing down his trousers, making sudden moves, or screaming, as it had been quite soft. Salcedo faced the shipmaster immediately, bringing the lamp a bit closer in order to see his visage better, which showed a stern look. His eyes were centered in their sockets, but it almost felt like he was trying to perceive what lurked behind them. The boy just stood there, waiting for Martín Alonso to somehow relay what he wanted him to do; the shipmaster eventually did, but, for some reason, it seemed he had taken forever. By shimmying his gaze to the left to meet Salcedo's, Martín Pinzón slightly moved his head inward, indicating he wanted the boy to turn around at the same time as him, therefore blinding and surprising whoever was waiting for them in the dark. On the shipmaster's mark, one he made clear by bulging his eyes, Salcedo turned and immediately extended the arm holding the lamp while the other held the sword horizontally, ready to pierce anyone willing to foil their plan; as for Martín Pinzón, he lifted his harquebus over the boy to avoid hitting him on his head with the gun's muzzle and swiftly took hold of the barrel again, firmly pointing it at the target. As it turns out, there was nothing there – they were safe. Only their labored breathing and the rusty squeak of the lamp produced sound, nothing more. The reason for the course of action the shipmaster had chosen to take was directly correlated with his feeling they were both being watched from the back, even if the ogler did not dispose of sufficient lighting to make out who the pair was. They eventually exhaled through their nose with relief, ready to keep moving aft through the remains of food scattered all over the floor. Salcedo's only hope for the moment was neither rats nor mice got in the way; judging from the size and especially color of their eyes, the boy could swear they were the devil's creation – they brought pestilence with them, which was what the Inferno was all about, so it is quite likely his assumption may be right in the end, their furless, fleshy tails to the likes of eerily haunting depictions of the rebel angel having one himself, whose tip resembled that of an arrow.

Having confirmed the passageway was clear, they kept walking, one step at a time, hoping a slow motion such as that could help minimize any other chances at future poor-tasted surprises, even though neither anyone nor anything had done so; the tiller was likely to be nearby, for they could already feel a nocturnal sea breeze blowing against their faces, though the shining stars in the horizon could not yet be seen through the gap Salcedo had come aboard. But it was not just about the rate of speed at which they moved, for, by advancing too slowly, the balance of the pair was subjected to instability, as it took longer to lower their feet's soles completely, beginning with the bluntness of the heel and only then exerting weight on the more adherent toes, despite their being inside shoes and, therefore, not in contact with the floor. With all the rotten rubbish spread across the orlop, stepping on food and perhaps making it ooze thick juice turned to poison was nearly next to impossible, even with a lamp, whose purpose was to illuminate at the height of the pair's eyes, not the surface they were walking on.

It just so happened that, not so surprisingly, Salcedo was about to literally set foot when his heel

Columbia: Part I

rested atop an irregular shape and made him trip to the side. The amount of noise was simply immeasurable – the few blades he was carrying on his back seemed like they had a voice of their own, crying out like aching infants. Out of sheer, dumb luck, if we may put it that way, he did not let go of the lamp – if he had, the vessel would have become a sailing sun in the night, burning every man on board, including the boy and the shipmaster.

Salcedo did not move; he was lying on his stomach over whichever object had betrayed him into falling but was able to remain still, except for the lamp, whose dangling was coming to an end, as was the squeak of the rusty hinges, begging for oil themselves. Martín Pinzón immediately knelt and pointed his harquebus forward as a means of prevention. It did not matter if everyone else was asleep and could not easily be woken up – the apparatus had been far too loud not to raise suspicion that something wrong was going on, and that was probably the reason why the pair heard footsteps immediately above, on the main deck. Their personal light source would not help contain the disaster, and so Martín Pinzón lay down close to Salcedo, whispering the following instructions to him:

'Take the chimney off and blow the flame out! Hurry!', which the boy did indeed.

They just stayed there, waiting to be captured,

though hopefully not without a fight, as the Moors had taught them by resisting endlessly to the Catholic Monarchs' incursions over the years. How long they lay in the dark without moving a muscle, no one can tell – not even them; what can be asserted without a doubt, however, is that no one descended the flight of stairs to perform any sort of inspection. The vessel could have been sinking, it did not matter, which was the kind of attitude a shipmaster could never feel proud of when it came to his sailors, though, at this particular time, Martín Pinzón thanked God for their carelessness.

After what it may have been a long while or no more than just a couple of minutes, Salcedo decided it was time to say something and possibly resume their plan, especially due to the discomfort he felt against his innards:

'Master Pinzón!', he whispered, 'Should we get up now...?'.

'Yes... I think so. It should be safe... it doesn't seem like anyone's coming...', the shipmaster whispered back, adding, 'what in blazes did you trip over, anyway? You were being so careful about your step...!'.

'I know, sir... I believe that might have just been the problem... I don't know what it was, but I can tell you it felt like I was lying on a piece of ham with its bone intact... Dios mío...!', Salcedo replied, ending his turn to speak with yet another

Columbia: Part I

concern, 'Now how do we light the burner again?'.

'Well, unless you've got a spare piece of flint in your pocket, we'll just have to rub a couple of blades together – but don't touch yours! You've made enough a racket as it is. Just let me feel where the burner is and… ah!, here we go', Martín Pinzón exclaimed, sensing the heat of the recently-put-out wick.

The shipmaster set down the harquebus on the floor and sought to produce friction with a pair of swords that up to that moment had been hanging from his back. Quietly bringing their edges together, Martín Pinzón employed a grinding motion he hoped would create a few sparks until the wick smoldered once more. It took between three to five tries, but he had done it – one of the sparks generated from the friction eventually landed where it should. Salcedo put the chimney back on the lamp and stretched out his right arm as the shipmaster pulled him up, back on his feet. In doing so, the boy sought balance with his left arm, the one whose hand he was using to hold the lamp, thus drifting it away from their center. After thanking Martín Pinzón for his help, Salcedo brought the light source closer yet again by retracting his forearm, revealing a few markings imprinted on his shirt he had not noticed before; in fact, had it not been for the shipmaster, the boy would have probably not realized they were there to begin with until much later. Martín Pinzón squinted and brought his left hand from the firearm's barrel to the boy's piece of apparel, trying to make out whether they were dry; as it turns out, however:

'Is this… fresh blood…?', the shipmaster whispered, 'Are you hurt?'.

'No, sir, I… I don't think so, no. I feel fine, but… now that you mention it, I believe this just might be blood, indeed…', Salcedo replied, looking down to his chest.

'That's a weird pattern, isn't it? It looks like a stripe, only… erratically punctured in places…', Martín Pinzón noticed, swabbing one of the dark-red stains with his index and bringing it closer to the lamp, concluding, 'it is blood… give me that lantern – I want to check something'.

Salcedo did as he was told and passed the lamp over to the shipmaster, who held it with his left hand as the other kept a firm grip on the harquebus; the man carefully crouched and slowly unveiled the horrible truth, the reason why his companion had tripped and fallen – a human leg lay on the floor, mangled to pieces. There was also a pool of blood marked on the floor, but it had already dried up, and that is why the imprint on both Salcedo's shirt and trousers near the waist area was far fainter. Shivers immediately ensued and flared down the boy's spine at the horrific sight; it was almost as if a satanic ritual had taken place, and right there, in the most impractical and uncommon of places – the insides of a ship, adrift somewhere on the surface of the uncharted and never-before-traveled Ocean Sea. Martín Pinzón proceeded with the examination, eventually uncovering the other leg, bent inward; it had also been chewed upon – at least up to where the shorts prevented any further revelations. There was no doubt both the shipmaster and the boy were in the presence of a body – they simply did not know yet whose it was. Martín Pinzón took a deep breath, showing disturbance on his face, and moved the lamp upward, from the dead man's torso (where rats were still having a feast, biting through the shirt and into the exposed bowels) to his neck, rigidly locked in a slight inclination back and to the left, almost as if it had been broken by another's hands.

Finally moving the light to his face, Martín Pinzón revealed the last ever facial expression life had enabled the man to emulate, and it was next to indescribable, but we will give it our best, despite its gore-filled, stomach-churning features: placed on his left shoulder was another rat whose anterior paws were placed on the victim's chin as to help itself stand, trying as hard as it could to pull out a piece of cloth he had been gagged with, seeking to gain access to the oral cavity, though the lower lip had already been munched upon; parts of the nostrils were missing and the eyes looked like they had overcome the lid barrier and been projected out of their sockets, not to mention one of them had its sclera pierced and was oozing down the right side of the neck, a dreadful spectacle the rodents seemed to have taken advantage of in order to satiate their hunger and quench their thirst. Apparently, the man had been deprived of his chances at fighting back and possibly squashing the creatures into mush one by one before they could have ever dreamt of climbing up his legs, given his hands were bound together behind his back with a sailor's hitch.

It is important to mention that, while the events of the previous paragraph take their bitter time to lay down on parchment, they most assuredly speed through any spectator's mind like thunder, which means that, as soon as Martín Pinzón revealed the brutality of what could have happened to Salcedo (had he not been instantly saved by the shipmaster) and that the dead man turned out to be the pilot, the boy jumped back against the ship's wall to the starboard side, producing the loudest racket as the swords hit each other, complemented by a lengthy, horrified scream. The force of impact also made at least one harquebus fire upward. Fortunately for Salcedo, his head escaped the path of the round, which penetrated the main deck, though it did miss him only by a couple of inches.

There was no turning back now – the Pinta's

entire crew had been rendered wide awake; voices began to spread all across the vessel and, even though the exact words could not be made clear because of everyone talking and running fore and aft simultaneously, struck by fear and turmoil, there was no doubt the staircase connecting the orlop to the main deck would soon be stomped by several mariners all at once. Martín Pinzón turned to Salcedo and told him, loudly:

'Go! Run to the stern and get out the way you came! Take those weapons and give them to my brothers and Colón any way you can! I'll try to hold them back for as long as possible'.

'But sir…!', Salcedo exclaimed, swiftly interrupted by the shipmaster:

'Don't make me say it again, boy! Just get out of here!', and so he did.

Salcedo grabbed the firearms and blades behind his back to help contain the draft they produced while he ran, eventually cutting himself in his right hand and forearm with the latter's edges, but that did not prevent him from keeping his cold blood, even though it was actually boiling. The path was shorter than he had initially thought, the night sky visible just a few feet away through the tiller gap. Without wasting any more time, he climbed the handle and crawled through to the rudder, crouching while holding his balance on the narrow surface to take hold of the towline, which he used to slide down to the nearby rowboat, burning his left hand from the friction, which inclusively began to fume because of the high speed. The boy landed in the cold water and was being quickly pulled down by the weight of his baggage, the reason why it was imperative for him to transfer everything into the boat, to which he was holding on, nearly capsizing it. His hands severely wounded, Salcedo was only able to secure part of the total number of blades and harquebuses he was carrying, as some of them broke free and traveled straight to the abyss, but the ones he had managed to save were enough for the officers trapped in La Gallega's cabin, who, in the meantime, had come back to the broken window to see what all the fuss was about. Columbus perceived the reflection of the guiding stars in the celestial dome glowing on the swords' blades and realized Salcedo had made it after all, looking back at the Pinzón brothers with a wide smile and again to the rowboat, ecstatically whispering:

'Córcholis! He's done it…!'.

Chapter V
Retribution

Francisco Martín Pinzón, master of the Pinta, was now fending all by and for himself against his fellow crewmen, threatening to shoot anyone who stood in his way as he sought to climb up to the main deck with one of his harquebuses primed and ready to fire:

'Away! Away with ye! Traitors! The Captain's done so much for you all over the years, now gives you a chance to come find a new reality, a new world, improve your livelihood and that of your offspring for generations to come... and this is how you repay him?! Scoundrels! Pigs of the abyss! 'Tis bile that flows in your veins in the stead of blood...! Such cruelty I could never have expected from you! You were my brothers as much as Martín and Vicente, not just sheer brethren! Now... if you truly call yourselves "men", if there is still a shred of honor inside you, help me rescue the Captain from that pissant de la Cosa's cowardly paws', the shipmaster passionately orated.

Some of the sailors exchanged gazes among them, unsure of the proper attitude to take, for there was conflict brewing in their hearts – on the one hand, a feeling of betrayal eloquently stated by Martín Pinzón; on the other, Juan de la Cosa's promise he would soon deliver them from the oceanic hell they currently found themselves in as if he were the very personification of Providence. Not everyone, however, felt as divided as did this particular group of sailors... two or three mariners had a few questions – literally:

'And why should we do that? There's nothing here for us but death', a first stated.

'Aye. If we push on, we might just hit land, but we won't be alive to see it', said another.

'Each day we spend here in the middle of nowhere, defying God's plan, is just another provocation, tempting Him to smite us as He conjures up a storm and wipes us out from this world as He did in the beginning of time. We'll all be fish fodder soon enough. Turning back is our only option if we ever wish to see our homes again, otherwise... there'll be no salvation from our sinning', a third noted, clearly convincing a great many others into murmuring just how right he was.

'You fool…', Martín Pinzón uttered, 'who do you think you are, pretending to be a priest preaching us all as if the Lord Himself spoke through you? If you were really that divinely enlightened, you'd know we don't have enough to make it back, even if the winds favored us the entire time, which clearly they don't', he continued, pointing with the firearm's muzzle to the main mast, whose sails were furled.

'Wind comes and goes, Pinzón – if we all ask for forgiveness, together, we might just achieve atonement', a voice projected from the fore section remarked; as the source walked toward the gathering, the shipmaster realized the words had been enounced by the Pinta's co-owner, Cristóbal Quintero, whose outlook was now more visible.

From behind and above, on the poop deck, another man made himself heard:

'And the moment we do, the Lord will blow into our sails toward safety, for which reason we began in the morning and will continue to do so by dawn', Gómez Rascón said, his hands resting on the taffrail, the background painted with the glow of stars, almost making him look ethereal, an angel come from the heavens specifically for the Annunciation.

The moment Rascón spoke his first word, the

shipmaster turned around and pointed his gun at him, discouraging the man from any sudden moves, which just happened to be the reaction of one of the sailors who had previously spoken, running toward Martín Pinzón with the intention of taking the harquebus away from him, but to no avail – the man with the weapons was vividly alert and heard the mariner's steps quickly approaching, hitting him in the nose and knocking him down with the firearm's butt. Now, given the inherent dangers of handling a piece of technology whose primary purpose was warfare and yet required a great deal of development safety-wise, it is really no surprise a shot was fired, injuring Rascón on his left arm, the echo flaring in every direction; shortly afterward, a clash of iron pieces sounded in the distance. Sure enough, it was but a flesh wound; still, any lacerations made to the human body, no matter how superficial, could easily turn into an amputated limb, as festering was almost always inevitable. The presence of gunpowder did not help, either. Rascón screamed in agony, instinctively held his arm with his opposite hand and collapsed on the poop deck floor. Quintero was immediately horrified, crying out his friend's name as he sought to break through the arc of men standing between him and Martín Pinzón, though they would not let him:

'Gómez! Gómez...! You killed him! Bastard!

Columbia: Part I

You killed him!

Before anyone else made other similarly foolish attempts bearing the same results, Martín Pinzón retrieved a second gun and pointed it to the encircling crowd, simultaneously issuing a warning:

'Stay back! Just stay back! Come any closer and I'll take you out right between your eyes…!'.

The men put their hands up and took a couple of steps back, dragging Cristóbal Quintero with them, still trying to escape the sailors' grasp and throw himself at the shipmaster, who attentively shimmied to port and climbed the stairs up to the poop deck, firmly holding the unused harquebus with both hands, putting the other one behind his back again. Martín Pinzón approached Gómez Rascón and saw he was squirming in pain, achingly gnashing his teeth after the first rolled the latter over with the aid of his foot.

'He's alive. Even if we have to chop his arm off, he'll still see daylight in the morning', he said, his gaze jumping from Rascón to Quintero, making sure once more the latter stayed where he should.

After a good amount of time spent looking at each other in silence, Martín Pinzón stopped pointing the harquebus at the crew and, taking his rightful place in Alonso Pinzón's stead as second-in-command, he faced the men and told them:

'My friends, I do not wish to harm any of you. All I'm doing is imploring you to see reason. We all knew what we were headed for once we left Palos. Uncertainty ruled with an iron fist. There was no telling for sure the exact distance between home and our objective. Then again, I also understand you've had enough, that it's been more than a month away from land – two, in fact, had it not been for the vessel's moronic proprietors, these two idiots', he said, pointing to Rascón and then Quintero, 'who made us stay away from our newly-reconquered country all this time by breaking their own ship in hopes we ceased and desisted, long before Colón brought us here. It's true, we are lost! No one knows how close the next isle is, but I can tell you this – attempting to sail back without restocking is suicidal. Even if we the wind does return tomorrow, it'll only blow against us, and we can't afford to make it all the way back by repeatedly beating and tacking. One of us is already dead!'.

The sailors looked at each other, trying to make out who was it that was missing, but neither of them reached any conclusions, making several simultaneously ask:

'Who?!'.

'Where is he?'.

'What happened...?'.

Martín Pinzón kept quiet, swallowing hard for

Columbia: Part I

a brief moment, finally satisfying the crew's curiosity:

'The pilot... he died earlier today. As to the remainder of your questions, he's below, on the orlop, serving as chow for the rats, and do you wish to know why...?', he rhetorically asked, as plenty drove their hands to their head with incredulity; the shipmaster then proceeded, 'Because he was exhausted and wanted to eat to help keep his mind awake and alert, but he couldn't – there's nothing left! Not even water! How do we survive without it...? If only we could throw a bucket overboard and heave it back up again with freshwater... but we can't... and you know it. If you don't believe me, go down and take as many lamps as possible, or you'll end up the same way that poor devil did'.

Willing to concede the shipmaster an opportunity to prove he had just given them his word, a couple of mariners unhooked a few lamps hanging from the aftercastle's wall, where Alonso Pinzón and Martín Pinzón himself retired to, and went down to the orlop, whereas others were still experiencing some difficulty buying his words, including none other than Cristóbal Quintero:

'He lies! You're lying, you despicable seadog! Even if the pilot really is dead, how can we be sure you didn't kill him and made it look like the rats did the job?!', he cried.

It was only at that moment that it came to

Martín Pinzón's mind the pilot's legs had been loosened, but not his hands, which both he and Salcedo had left tied up. However, there was this longshot hope inside him that the rodents could've chewed through the line by now, releasing the dead man's hands. While everyone waited for the return of the impromptu search party, the shipmaster continued to eloquently orate, attempting to sway as many sailors as he could into reinstating him as the authority in the Captain's absence:

'Hold your tongue, Quintero…! Do you realize how barbaric you make me sound?! Slaying one of our own just to prove a point?! That's de la Cosa's train of thought, and so is yours! You're in league with him, so it's really not that much of a surprise, is it…? Your pride is hurting so that you just had to take over, despite the means to your end! It's true what the folk say… the devil does make work for idle hands'.

As Quintero prepared to retort, trembling light could be seen growing in intensity as the men returned from below. They had gone alone, but that was not the case now – as the first ascended, it became clear he was holding a pair of legs whose sight was too atrocious to bear, even in the middle of the night, despite the stars' luminosity; the second sailor soon followed, holding a pair of arms as high as possible, trying to avoid hitting the stairs with something apparently swinging like dead weight in the middle of said limbs. It is no wonder that is what it resembled, as the mariners were bringing the pilot's dead body with them, having lain it on the deck floor for everyone to see, including Gómez Rascón, who was still lying next to Martín Pinzón in pain, eventually rolling over on himself to take a better look. As soon as they let go of the corpse, the two self-appointed envoys ran across the deck and hurled strongly, all the way to rendering their throats hoarse. As for the others, all sorts of repulsed exclamations were cried out:

'Dios mío!'.

'No puede ser…!'.

'Caray, que chiste!'.

'Ay!, guácala…!'.

As disgusted as he was to ogle the pilot's body a second time, even though it was from afar this time, Martín Pinzón could not help but feel relieved to see the rodents had indeed chomped the line holding the dead man's hands together to smithereens, which meant any signs of wrongdoing possibly attributed to him were off the table – an important factor contributing to the further inflammation of his speech:

'And there you have it, lads…! Behold the dreadful spectacle! Do you see now what awaits you once your legs give out…?! Even if you're still alive by just a thread, they'll come for you! You can't possibly tell me this is how you want to end up, even if no one ever finds us…! Please, I beg of you… this is no order from the shipmaster… it is a humble request – save us all from an ending such as this and come about…'.

Gazing at Cristóbal Quintero in search of feedback while simultaneously avoiding the ominous display lying there at their feet at any cost, the crew waited for the former's instructions, though he failed to give any. Next to Martín Pinzón, Gómez Rascón attempted to get up with a great deal of effort involved, holding on to the taffrail with his good arm while applying force to his legs in order to stand. The shipmaster noticed the movements, but did not prevent the vessel's co-owner from pursuing his objective, which he only attained by half, leaning against the taffrail with both his stomach and right forearm, applying pressure once more with his right hand to the bleed on his injured limb. Without looking at Martín Pinzón and with his eyes fixated on the pilot, Rascón gave out the order, but not without some difficulty:

'You heard the Master… prepare to drop sail and… come about, but only… only after we pay our respects to our comrade and… release the Captain. Either we all turn around to safety, or no one does'.

The moment he finished talking, he ogled Martín Pinzón at last, exuding confidence in him despite the stern expression; one had just shot the

Columbia: Part I

other, after all, speaking of which, yet another firearm round was heard on the starboard side, likely coming from the Santa María and followed by a splash.

***

During the events taking place aboard the Pinta, the Santa María was too involved, with Salcedo playing the part of the protagonist while Columbus and the Pinzón brothers, Vicente Yáñez and Martín Alonso, were watching the ship's boy giving it his best to return to the vessel with the weapons he had managed to collect from the Pinta's hull with the aid of Francisco Martín, despite losing some of them to the depths only a few moments before.

The round Columbus's personal servant had inadvertently fired from the Pinta's orlop the moment he saw the pilot's rodent-defiled body had not just been heard aboard the vessel formerly captained by Alonso Pinzón – on the contrary, it eventually spread across the Ocean Sea surface, though faintly. Still, a few crewmen aboard the flagship were compelled to stay alert, unaware, however, of the sound's source, rendering them confused. One could ask oneself what is it with the Niña's mariners for them to not care one bit about all these developments taking place on the decks of the other vessels, but the fact the ship in question was slightly more adrift to starboard, having followed its own rhythm throughout the whole day as the fastest of the three, would just have to work as the ultimate excuse, regardless of how extraordinarily speculative it might sound.

Pedro de Salcedo's first instinct the moment he sat on the rowboat was to stand again and cut the towline loose from its bow with the use of a blade; because it was somewhat thick, it took two to three slaying instances until the rope was finally severed. Soon after taking care of that teeny snag, he sat down for good and took hold of the boat's other oar, the one the boy had chosen to leave behind when first attempting to board the Pinta. It was far more difficult to steer with only one paddle available, having to push the water back on both sides in order to move ahead in a straight line, but if he had made it that far on his mission, it was not going to be the lack of another oar stopping him from attaining success.

Columbus could be seen above, at the Santa María's portside window, effusively encouraging Salcedo to keep rowing:

'Órale, boy! You're so close…! Come along, now… that's right – just keep on pushing!'.

With remarkably great effort, the ship's boy, having his hands severely wounded and feeling tired from a long day of physical antics (given that all he had done so far regarding exercise had simply been walking fore and aft, relaying messages between the Admiral's cabin and the royal officials' forecastle quarters), made it to La Gallega, stationing the rowboat right beneath the window. He then looked up and uttered not without some difficulty:

'Admiral...! I'm here... I told you I'd gladly give up my life if I had to, but not before delivering you from your ordeal... I have swords and guns... now how do I bring them up?'.

Yáñez Pinzón quickly came up with a solution, heading for Columbus's bed to retrieve the sheets and any other layers he could find with the purpose of making a line from them for Salcedo to climb. Alonso Pinzón, having realized what his brother was up to, also sought to help out, despite the obvious poor lighting problem. The Admiral also understood what the brothers' intention was when he turned his head back, turning it forward and down again to tell the boy the Captains were taking care of it:

'Don't worry! We have a line for you... well, sort of, but it'll do, just hang tight...!'.

'Yes, sir...!', Salcedo said with a smile, perhaps figuring it was one way to cope with the pain; of course, the fact the only plan to take him up was for him to climb and, therefore, make use of his slit hands was not something to look forward to, but he was sure the Admiral would let him rest and even commend him after all he had done in the course of a little over half a day for approximately ninety men, including himself.

Having both made sure the knots could not be easily unfastened, Yáñez and Alonso Pinzón ran to the broken window and threw the makeshift line, hopefully within Salcedo's reach, which would only be possible if they held it themselves, considering there was nothing heavier in the cabin to secure it to. As for Columbus, he kept watch, ready to grab Salcedo's hand as soon as possible, helping him and the goodies he brought with him inside, but things were not looking so good.

Salcedo put the weapons behind his back all at once, making him nearly double his weight; speedily inhaling and exhaling, the boy spat in his palms, crouched and then jumped as high as he could, grabbing the first sheet close to knot connecting it to the next. This abrupt shift in the amount of strength necessary to hold the line made the Pinzón brothers quickly slide simultaneously against the cabin wall, bulging their eyes with surprise at first, followed by gnashing their teeth to hold on, inclusively applying force to the wall with their feet, as if it were possible for them to walk vertically, which is none other than what Salcedo considered would be easier for him as well; in order to provide better support on his way up, he placed his feet against the ship's side and started walking while it seemed, from an entirely different perspective, he was falling – except he was going the opposite way, thus defying some kind of universal principle no one had yet successfully managed to explain.

As he kept climbing, Salcedo faintly released a few aching sounds, leaving a trail behind him tainted with both blood and necrotic skin from his right and left hands, respectively.

When the boy was about halfway up, a rifle round was fired, echoing behind and startling not just him, but also the three men locked in the cabin – it had undoubtedly come from the Pinta, though the exact circumstances leading to the event could not be perceived in their entirety due to a lack of lighting; we already know it was the product of Martín Pinzón's self-defense against the crewman who had tried to take his gun away, accidentally shooting Gómez Rascón in his arm in the aftermath, but they did not. Still, it was enough to make Salcedo lose both his focus and grip, consequently falling on his back and into the rowboat, breaking the aftmost thwart strut; even though the boy could not wait for this day to be over, his luck had not abandoned him completely, as he could have been easily diced by the blades he was carrying or poked an orifice in the boat with either a sword or another shot from a harquebus (or more, even), losing the only platform he could hold on to before drowning.

Up in the cabin, both Yáñez and Alonso Pinzón obviously fell as well, though not high enough to injure themselves; the loss of the counterweight on the other side of the makeshift line generated by Salcedo and his weapons could not hold them to the wall anymore to make it look like they were standing on it. Martín Alonso was the one asking the predictable question, preceded by a colorful interjection:

'Caray…! What happened…?!'.

'He fell!', Columbus exclaimed without looking away from the boy below, asking him, 'Are you all right, Salcedo?!'.

'Madre mía…!', he said, facing the sky and pretty much wishing he could soon be taken there in the shape of a star so he could be put out of his misery once and for all; his resilience, however, which was none other than a gift from God, prevented him from leaving his body, mustering every breath to rise and grab that line again, telling the Admiral, 'I'm fine, Don Cristóbal…! Do you know what happened…?!'.

'I think it came from the Pinta', Columbus replied.

Alonso Pinzón had not yet realized there was a good chance the Admiral just might be right. He got back up on his feet and threw Salcedo the line again as he was joined by Yáñez Pinzón, asking the latter:

'Could it be Francisco…?'.

'I certainly hope so… otherwise, it'll only make it more difficult for us to get out of this mess – which by now is beyond messy, to tell you the truth…', Yáñez Pinzón confessed.

'Come now, gentlemen…', Columbus began to tell them, 'we're not going back to Castile – not today and not without a damned good fight, which is far more important! Vaya, Salcedo! Try again, son! Almost done, almost done…!'.

The Admiral's words of encouragement did move the boy indeed, and quite literally. He set his feet on La Gallega's side and walked vertically a second time, repeatedly tainting the sheets with markings from his open wounds. Each step he took, however, was beginning to take something for itself, and that was a large toll, ruthlessly extracted from Salcedo's body; the ugly truth is words can only mean and boost so much when faced with real live action. He paused for a moment, struggling for air to soothe the pain he was feeling all over; falling on your back and breaking a wooden board is usually bound to do further damage, and this was precisely the case in point – the boy had likely broken a couple of ribs, if not an extended number. Incapable of moving any further, he came up with a workaround, which was handing the weapons one by one to Columbus.

'There's no other way, Admiral... I can't keep going...! Just take them! Come back for me when you can... I'll be waiting... take them, please...!'.

Columbus swallowed hard with reluctance, but he gave it his best to reach the firearms' butts and the swords' hilts. As we have realized by now, there were no scabbards to seclude the blades; each crewman carried his own, though they had been empty this far to avoid any confrontations – an outcome that found its way in between them all, anyway, for such is human nature.

For Salcedo, this meant holding the blades' central ridges as best as he could without cutting himself any more than he already had, but to nearly no avail; without a firm grip, the swords would just keel over and into the Ocean Sea, rendered perpetually lost. The boy extended his arm as far as it would reach while single-handedly holding on to the nearest knot in the line. In turn, Columbus performed his part also and leaned over the window while trying himself to avoid getting cut from the glass remains.

'That's it...! Raise it... just raise it a bit higher! Can you pull him up just a little more?', he asked the Pinzón brothers, who looked like they were going to break a blood vessel around their temples.

'You ask too much, Colón...! Have you ever noticed that...?!', Yáñez Pinzón remarked, strangling himself as he spoke in order for the Admiral to hear him clearly.

Applying the strength reserves they both had left, the Pinzón brothers heaved Salcedo no more than a couple of inches more – just about enough to bring the swords within range of Columbus's hand. Only two made it successfully into the cabin. The boy was sure he was packing more, but that was all there was.

'Never mind!', Columbus exclaimed, 'These are enough for now. Send in the guns!'.

Salcedo followed his master's instruction as promptly as possible and passed him a harquebus while holding it by the muzzle, unavoidably pointed at him. In turn, the Admiral caught grip of the weapon's butt, pulling it with a slight hop until he held it close to the trigger, and that is when it all went terribly awry. In a matter of only a fraction of a second, Salcedo's eyes were locked in place as they would be until time eroded them away, his gaze fixated in another's, illuminated for as long as it took the ship's boy to slightly turn his head to his left and leave it there as one final warning delivered to the Admiral, eventually taking a plunge with a hole in his chest, gushing blood onto Columbus's expression of incredulity. The latter knew it could not have been him firing the round – the gun had not jerked in his hand, there was no smoke coming out of the muzzle, no recoil, nothing. Bearing Salcedo's hint in mind before falling to his death, Columbus turned to his right and saw the ugly truth – Juan de la Cosa was the murderer. The harquebus he was holding was still puffing out smoke when he threw it on the quarterdeck floor and grabbed another one already loaded, this time aiming for the Admiral's head. Columbus, though visibly in shock, managed to find the nerve that would save him from being summarily executed right there and, quickly leaning the palm of his hands against the wall, he pushed back and fell over the Pinzón brothers, who were already lying on the floor again due to the sudden loss of counterweight. Splinters were seen bursting out of the windowsill, accompanied by both a flash and a bang coming from the right.

'What the hell was that?!', Alonso Pinzón cried out.

'De la Cosa...!', Columbus exasperated, rubbing his face with his left hand while holding the harquebus with his right, only to see blood on the palm – Salcedo's blood.

'What?!', Yáñez Pinzón intervened.

'It's de la Cosa! He killed Salcedo and tried to shoot me just now! Get up! Get up! Up, up, up! Grab those blades and prepare to attack! I'll get the door!', Columbus shouted, foaming out of his mouth with tremendous rage.

His heart racing and the rest of his body trembling, the Admiral was still capable of aiming the rifle at the lock, destroying it beyond repair with a powerful burst.

'Dai, dai, dai! Chop him to pieces!'.

The Pinzón brothers wielded their swords while Columbus opened the door with the harquebus's muzzle. As the three came running out the cabin, they also ran into an encircling firing squad – several crewmen were holding harquebuses and aiming them at the officers, who felt nothing short of stumped. They were standing right on the quarterdeck, close enough to shoot point-blank.

De la Cosa, who had been leaning from the staircase going up that level to get a good aim at Salcedo and, soon after, Columbus, finished climbing the steps and approached, dropping the used firearm on the floor while bearing a ridiculous-looking grin on his face.

'Who would've thought you could still amaze me, Colón…?'.

'I'm glad you're impressed', Columbus snarkily retorted.

'There, you see…? You ruin it all with your salty seadog wit. I was making a reference to your gullibility. You make a boy do all your dirty work and expect to take credit for his bravery. Aye… this is the real you', de la Cosa said.

'I'm sure Yáñez and Alonso Pinzón are willing to testify on my behalf just how much I encouraged Salcedo to find help in any possible way he could',

Columbus began to say, adding in a crescendo, 'and reward him as soon as he proved himself successful, which he was about to, had you not gratuitously put him down like a common beast!'.

'He was aiding the enemy – on my ship. He was a traitor and was dealt with as such'.

'Ma che diavolo...! How dare you?! Good God, man! The only traitor here is you! This isn't just my enterprise...! We're all here in the name of Queen Isabella! You're preventing a royal venture from happening! The Crown spent tremendous sums of money over the years fighting the unfaithful – the country needs to profit! We're losing trade to the Portuguese! They keep exploring, making tens of thousands of sovereigns per exchange, collecting allies all over, buying slaves as personal servants and a nationwide workforce... and what have we got? Nothing! We don't have the money to pay the taxes they demand in Lisbon for spices! I know – I used to live there; I know how much they cost!', Columbus orated, looking not just at de la Cosa, but also the rest of the men, seeking to make them see moving forward would be worth their while in the end.

'No, no, no... don't do that, Colón... don't go looking for feedback in my men's eyes to support your cause. We were half-assing our lives just fine without all these aspirations of yours, like becoming rich overnight without even knowing what

Columbia: Part I

you're doing. Thank God for casting heavenly light into my soul… one day sailing back home may have just made all the difference', de la Cosa heroically remarked.

'You complete, utter imbecile…! It's too late to turn back! Must I hammer the concept into your wooden noggin?! We've no food left! Yes, I know, we packed too light for such a long journey, and yes, I know, I miscalculated the numbers, but the mist at dawn was a sign we were already there! Five, ten leagues more… couldn't have we survived it?! Would you rather go around the whole of Africa like the neighbors? Even if you did, there'd be a blockade somewhere along the way to hold you captive and sink your ship', Columbus further discoursed in outrage.

'Well, you see…?! We finally agree! My ship, it's my ship – not yours, not the Queen's, and definitely not the country's. As long as I can put food on my table every day, I don't care about your delusions of grandeur. You want to come back here again? Fine. Do it on your own time, with your own vessel, crewed by your own people. In the meantime, you're joining the nobility down in the hull', de la Cosa implacably stated.

'You can't possibly expect to get out of this unpunished… you'll be sentenced to death! All of you! For murdering an innocent boy and placing royally appointed officers under arrest', Columbus shouted, facing every man involved in the never-before-seen act of treason, adding still, 'not to mention financially compromising the Crown and the investments of so many others whose future depends on the success of this enterprise. I can see how the business side of things might be irrelevant to you, my good man, but there's a great deal more to this than just dropping sails and steering a damned rudder... but you know what? Fine – have it your way. You just go ahead and take us straight home. I trust your seaman skills to keep us at bay from the eye of a typhoon, avoid a storm, or even come up with brand-new food and drink storages on the way. I'm sure we'll all be alive to see you be welcomed back like a hero for saving everyone from thirst and starvation. After all, it's only been a month and a week since we left the Canary Islands... with the winds favoring us, of course. Good luck tacking all the way there'.

This is exactly how Columbus always managed to persuade those around him. It is not the first time we witness it – both Yáñez and Alonso Pinzón were equally swayed effortlessly. The self-taught Genoese patron of the local Cordobese apothecary could simultaneously handle several jobs at once, whether it be navigator, explorer, astronomer, geographer, cartographer, mathematician, interpreter, what have you – but when it came to convincing someone to join him, he just pulled

Columbia: Part I

it off flawlessly. Juan de la Cosa had not fallen for the Italian's number up until then, he certainly was not going to fall now. The crewmen, however, they were swapping gazes, silently polling each other. They still had their harquebuses pointed at the Admiral and the two Captains, but it somehow felt like the firmness with which they had held them so far was progressively fading away; the problem was... who would dare lower them first?

De la Cosa, of course, had something more to say:

'We're not headed for the Canaries, Colón... the Azores are closer. We berth there. As for you, I never said you'd be alive to see us drop anchor. I never even said you'd be aboard that long. Your charming, silver-real words may be rhetorically interesting, but they won't save you. On the contrary – you've only made my decision easier. You let me worry about the story we'll tell the Queen; what she doesn't know won't hurt her. Lads! Prepare to fire'.

While some of the mariners were switching their upper body support from one leg to another, blinking repeatedly so as to improve their visual acuity, others did not even flinch. We must not forget there were criminals among the crew, former convicts with nothing to lose; if they could shoot the man responsible for their being adrift God-knows-where and come up with a cover story sponsored by the shipmaster himself, thus acquitting themselves of any possible charges for lack of evidence, then why not do it straight away? He was right in front of them – all they had to do was squeeze the trigger.

On the opposite side, still holding on to the used harquebus and their swords, Columbus and the Pinzón brothers, respectively, slowly crouched to put down their weapons, recovering at the same rate of speed. None of them intended to provoke the sailors who might be feeling nervous about any sudden moves from the officers – not that it would do the latter any good, bringing blades to a gunfight, but there was still a good chance of hitting and missing on the mariners' part. The Admiral did not have any more cards up his sleeve; he had already stated the facts the way they were, for which reason the only thing left to do was to commend his spirit into the Lord's hands, raising his own toward the sky as he closed his eyes. Yáñez and Alonso Pinzón looked at each other for a moment and, having no other choice, did exactly the same as Columbus, the three of them simultaneously mouthing in prayer.

Juan de la Cosa took a few steps back to avoid being accidentally hit and, with his arms behind his back and his fingers intertwined, gave the order step by step:

'Guns at the ready'.

Columbia: Part I

The three targets began to show a pained expression, as if they were preparing, if not hardening their bodies to endure the piercing of several cast lead bullets just waiting for a small explosion in the harquebuses' barrels to project them.

'Take aim'.

The second stage; both Columbus and the Pinzón brothers closed their eyes shut, making it look like they would have to be pried open with iron crows even after their souls and willpower abandoned the flesh-and-bone carcasses God had created for them to live in before rejoining him in Heaven.

One more word and that was it. They would already be dead by the time the shipmaster finished crying out the execution order's final stage – there is always a trigger-happy lunatic in this sort of situation who cannot wait to feel empowered by taking another's life.

It is a well-known fact plenty of people at the verge of their death reportedly stop interpreting the environment they find themselves in just before they depart, both visually and auditorily, regardless of the physical condition their eyes and ears may be in during that particular moment, only to focus on a speedy replay of the most significant times of their life, and all that inside their mind. It was something like this that was currently taking place in both Columbus and the Pinzón brothers' memory slots, wherever in the brain they may be. Randomly choosing one of the three for the purposes of a better illustration, the Admiral returned to an instance he had memorized as the first he had set his eyes on the sea; being a Genoese by birth, it was like fate had prepared him to be in touch with great bodies of salt water concealing the unknown throughout his entire life, beginning with none other than the Ligurian.

The images that followed took the young Italian explorer-to-be to Lisbon, where he had settled as a cartographer with his brother, Bartholomew, anxious to start sailing as far as he could, concocting the enterprise together with his sibling, the same venture that had now seen its rather premature ending. Though there was a certain bittersweet taste to those moments because of the constant rejection from several European powers, including the Portuguese Crown, whose role in what had become the «Age of Discovery» was of the utmost importance and, therefore, made João II the perfect patron, his future success in swaying the Catholic Monarchs of Castile and Aragon made it all even better, especially because he got to be the leader of the expedition, the biggest achievement of his life only second to the birth of his children, Diogo and Fernando, both entitled to bear his name and continue his legacy, looking out for Beatriz once he left this world, which he did not intend to do so soon;

unfortunately, however, his time had come.

Pretending to be an actual officer of the Navy, de facto relieving the Admiral of his command and assuming his position, Juan de la Cosa drove his right arm forward and lifted it, bringing it down as he yelled:

'Fire!'.

The three officers, set to be put down like beasts, trembled; their legs nearly gave in, but the truth is they were still standing, burying their eyes deep into their sockets while their jaws mutually bit each other, applying pressure on their teeth nearly as strong as that of dogs, for lack of another animal they knew could be more powerful in comparison.

What had happened after all? Apparently… nothing. The triggers were squeezed, the locks hit the breeches, but no ammunition was projected out of the lengthy barrels.

Those who had attempted to fire (considering some eventually gave up in the middle of the executionary process) tried squeezing the trigger again and again, but to no avail – the harquebuses were simply not loaded. We know two of them, the ones used by de la Cosa to shoot down Salcedo and attempt on Columbus's life, had fired without showing any resistance whatsoever, but all others… rendered useless just like that.

Dazed and confused, the would-be murderers

were far too distracted trying to figure out what had gone wrong, not caring for the Admiral or the Captains at all. It was too good an opportunity to miss. With his eyes wide open once more, Columbus took hold of Alonso Pinzón's sword, ran to and pointed it at de la Cosa's neck, who was as dumbstruck as everyone else, unable to find the time to react against the Admiral's offensive. As for the others, Vicente Yáñez swiftly grabbed his blade from the floor while Martín Alonso caught the harquebus; it had to be cleaned and reloaded before it could fire again, but the sailors were not sure anymore. Either way, it was enough for them to stand down.

'I could slay you right here and now...', Columbus whispered, to the shipmaster's horrified expression, 'no one – no one, I tell you, would ever dare stop me, let alone think about it'.

De la Cosa swallowed hard, his gulp descending ever-so close to the tip of the blade, risking being throated at his own convenience. As per the laws of retribution, the tables had turned once more, thus restoring balance to the universe, obliterating chaos – that was the civilized route to take, after all.

'But you're not worth it', the Admiral continued, 'which is why I'll let Lady Justice set your fate in stone. I can't imagine how happy the Inquisition will be when they find out you tried to stop the

One Faith from spreading to other corners of the world. They will eat you up, chew you, and spit you back out again. Your head will be severed and put through a spike to set the example'.

De la Cosa took his left hand from behind his back and, together with his right, which was already alongside his torso, lifted them close to his face, shivering at every step along the way, especially when Columbus thought he was about to do something stupid such as grabbing the blade, only making the Admiral force the point deeper into his neck, eventually making him bleed, though the cut was not at all serious – for the time being, anyway.

'Please... I beg of you... let us converse, Don Cristóbal... Almirante... I'm sure we can reach some sort of agreement, erm... make a pact, perhaps!', de la Cosa exclaimed, his voice weaselly breaking.

'Don't bother, scum! "Your charming, silver-real words may be rhetorically interesting, but they won't save you. On the contrary – you've only made my decision easier". I'm never forgetting those words... you've brought this upon yourself, scum of the seas', Columbus retorted, delighted at the sight of de la Cosa's cowardness.

He, who had admonished a couple of sailors not many hours ago for pissing against the wind, which, in turn, had blown their waste onto the deck, was the one who ended up wetting himself.

Disgusted, the Admiral stepped back, pulling the blade away from de la Cosa's bleeding neck and turned around just so he did not have to look at his face.

'Gr-Gracias, Don Cristóbal... gracias... you are unmistakably merciful, indeed...', the poor devil uttered, falling on his knees and on a puddle of his own urine, though he spoke much too soon; finally able to relieve all the tension and anger that had built up inside him since the morning, Columbus turned again and struck de la Cosa in his face with the sword's pommel, rendering him unconscious. Luckily, he missed his piss.

The Admiral stood there looking at him with mixed feelings of repugnance and sadness, not because he felt sorry for de la Cosa himself, but rather because of how conformist and servile Man could be when faced with the possibility of broadening Humanity's horizons.

Closely watching the scene from the Pinta's deck, Francisco Martín Pinzón and the rest of the crew signaled their availability to help enforce a bit of order, to which Columbus agreed by gesturing "by all means", thus inviting the middle Pinzón brother and some of his men to board La Gallega, take the treacherous de la Cosa and the frustrated shooters siding with him down to the hull, put them in chains, and release the royally appointed officials, including the master-at-arms, chosen by

Columbia: Part I

the Admiral himself, of course – Diego de Arana, whose contributions to the rifles' misfiring would most assuredly renew the Admiral's trust in him. Without lengthening the episode, suffice it to say that, as was implied in the designation of his role, Arana was the one responsible for the armament and, just as much as the crew had been rendered weaponless to avoid something like this long episode of mutiny and insubordination, so were the harquebuses stored below without any gunpowder. In the end, the bullets had always been there, in the barrels, locked in place; however, without that essential ingredient the Moors had come up with for a few centuries, now, there was no possible way to fire them and mortally wound any targets at all, who or whatever they were.

This Diego de Arana came to explain to Columbus once he was freed and they both had a chance to hold each other again, making sure the other was all right. As for the Captains, both Vicente Yáñez and Alonso Pinzón greeted their brother Francisco Martín, happy to see he too was fine; having kept his mead nearby all day long, there is just no way he could not be – in fact, it may have even improved his judgment regarding this immense ordeal. He certainly would not be the first to attribute the success of a well-done deed to alcohol.

Before everyone retired to their bunks, the

rowboat Pedro de Salcedo had used not long before to put an end to the rebellion was reattached to the Pinta's stern; the boy's corpse, however, was no longer in sight. Columbus would have wanted to cast the body in the sea all the same, though with dignity and respect, instead of just leaving it behind with that unforgettable expression of betrayal spread across his face. Given that it was impossible to perform those rites, they were only applied to Pinta's pilot's body, wrapped inside the stained sheets Salcedo had tried to climb to reach the Santa María's cabin, thus associating both martyrs to the same sacrifice. Of course, only Martín Pinzón knew about the real connection between the two crewmen, but because it was so ugly and would only stain the memory of the victims (Salcedo's, especially), he kept his mouth shut – not to mention doubt would fall all over him, which was not at all suitable for someone who had just hoped to pin the pilot's death on the rats thriving in all three vessels, successfully attaining said objective. Having the prayers come to an end, the corpse was placed on a wooden board, taken to the Pinta's stern, and jetted into the Ocean Sea, quickly disappearing while it made its way down the abyss.

Two ships away to starboard, Yáñez Pinzón had at last returned to the Niña, waking everyone up with incredulity lurking behind every sound he uttered as he admonished his supposed comrades,

Columbia: Part I

brandishing his sword with an extraordinary amount of both rage and annoyance for the crew's inactivity and stoicism, willing to just leave their Captain in La Gallega's cabin to rot. While what he told them was rather unclear, we know for sure no one dared defy his authority ever again, apparently coming to an understanding with Juan Niño and the others.

The last event of the evening took place a few moments later, bringing a great deal of noise with it – a flock of what seemed to be terns (which probably pertained to the same family as seagulls, judging from their outlook) flew in an oncoming direction, squawking intensely as they passed over the mariners' heads, much to their amazement.

Most naturally, the once frustrated Admiral was no longer feeling dead inside; life itself had just come to enlighten him, painting a wide smile on his tired-looking visage, though reminding him also of what he had learned from Portuguese ventures to the like of his own – birds flying over the surface could only mean one of two things: they were either migrating to nearby land, where the weather was far more appealing than whence they came, or they were simply returning from a short fishing trip, headed back home with their stomachs full for the night. One way or another, everyone had just witnessed how right the Admiral had always been; coming about would have turned out to be the worst mistake of those sailors' lives, ever-so close to finding new horizons, or a "new world", as Columbus himself had put it, allowing their names to forever remain inscribed in the tomes of History, as they were now sure to live to tell the tale.

Come the morning, the first thing to do needed not be verbalized, but we shall do it all the same, for the sake of the literary device – drop sail and turn the tillers as far as they would go; somewhere there was a beach to find.

Chapter VI
Land-ho!

Over the following four days, up to the eve of the twelfth, the flotilla sailed with extraordinary smoothness. Having gotten back on track, the winds were blowing favorably and signs of proximity to land began to make themselves seen, with more birds flying in, namely sandpipers, which were waders and, therefore, did not drift far away from terra firme.

Still, there was the question of the agreement Columbus had made with both Yáñez and Alonso Pinzón – just a few hours more and it would expire, which is somewhat difficult to comprehend, given the recent life-threatening events the Captains had gone through together with the Admiral.

Such is the nature of humans and, consequently, our people skills – one will both usually and swiftly value the worst in detriment of the best, not even thinking twice about questioning the prevailing forces for good, as a small mistake made while wandering about an erroneous path outshines everything else, no matter how short a time one spends treading it, eventually acknowledging one was wrong to boot. In this particular situation, however, we are not condoning the idea that Columbus and the Pinzón brothers being trapped nearly a whole day inside La Gallega's cabin is something to be proud of – quite the contrary; nevertheless, the fact they had all those hours to bond and build a united front against de la Cosa's failed attempt at a coup should have brought them closer together. Their lives had been at stake and nothing about it had yet changed, inspiring both Yáñez and Alonso Pinzón to wave their fingers at the Admiral, almost demanding that he magically produce land as quickly as possible, under penalty of coming about, which was an obviously ridiculous, if not senseless threat; if on the seventh it was already too late to turn back, how could engaging in the same idea after sailing West for nearly five extra days not be counterproductive? Over a hundred more leagues had been traveled during that time – that was it; they might as well slit their throats open all at once if they did not mean to keep heading for

Columbia: Part I

Cipango.

There was no more evidence Columbus could produce to convince them land was near. The mist kept thickening each morning, there was vegetation bearing fruit, and all the more birds kept flying over their heads, leaving several markings on the deck floor as they passed, which the Admiral found to be rather amusing, much unlike the sailors in charge of mopping. Naturally, it was far worse when the men were hit. Throwing a bucket of salt water over themselves might have been purifying, but the growing heat of the circling Sun was tremendously impacting the mariners regarding their skin condition, making them look as if they had been put in a cauldron at boiling temperature, rendered red and peeling everywhere.

At around ten in the evening, Columbus, standing on La Gallega's poop deck, thought he had seen something interesting not far from the flotilla's position, close enough for his visual range to perceive it, of course; the problem, though, was he failed to be sure he had in fact caught eye of what he considered a flame-like phenomenon, ordered to dance to the sound of the wind, like a wax candle, rising and falling. Fearing his sight might be deceiving him, he called upon Pedro de Terreros and ordered him to get Pedro de Gutiérrez from the forecastle to seek confirmation. Once the royal steward stepped outside toward the midships, the

Admiral immediately addressed him:

'Señor Mayordomo! Would you join me up here, por favor?'.

'On my way, Señor Colón!', the official replied.

The man climbed the quarterdeck stairs on the portside and approached Columbus, who then posed the question with both his right index and his eyes fixed on the spot where light had shone:

'Do you see that there…?'.

Gutiérrez aimed his sight at the spot in the horizon Columbus was pointing to, but failed to discern any shapes:

'I'm sorry, Admiral, but I can't say that I do… what is it that I'm looking for, exactly?'.

Excited he had definitely found something, the Italian's eyes did not dare lose sight of the flame, though he did not wish to influence the steward into seeing something that could still be just some sort of mirage, similar to those in the desert, when the severe heat and dehydration combined compromise one's judgment. Instead, Columbus placed himself behind Gutiérrez and rested his extended arm on the steward's right shoulder, making for a better aim at the spot in question.

'There! Do you see it?! Can you make something out of it…?!'.

The Mayordomo moved his head slightly and followed the imaginary trail Columbus's finger projected, blinking three or four times to improve his acuity. It was then it hit him; given he was behind him, Columbus could not see the full extent of the steward's facial expression as his eyes bulged and his mouth was rendered half-open.

'W-What is that…? It-it can't be… or can it…? I…', Gutiérrez stammered, 'it looks like… maybe a torch, or something… but there's no way to be sure'.

'But you did see it, right?! Something up ahead, like moving light, huh?! I need Sánchez up here. Terreros! Fetch me the Comptroller – at once!', the Admiral exclaimed.

'Aye, sir – straight away', the cabin's boy responded.

Again, as Rodrigo Sánchez came out of the forecastle, Columbus called him up to the poop deck. The moment the official stood next to the Mayordomo, the Admiral asked him:

'Don Rodrigo, do you see movement up ahead, behind the mist? A light source shivering, perhaps…?'.

'Erm… where, exactly…? Can you point towa- oh!, thank you very much, indeed', he said, interrupted by Columbus when he was about to request that the Admiral indicate the spot with better precision, the latter eventually doing the same he had done with Gutiérrez, firmly extending his index finger as he rendered Sánchez uncomfortable from the lack of space Columbus was leaving between them.

To the like of Gutiérrez, the Comptroller was experiencing difficulties making anything out of the darkness in the horizon, something he ended up confessing to:

'No... I regret I see nothing, Señor Colón... "shivering light", you say? Hmm...', he uttered, driving his right hand to his beard, scratching it pensively as the elbow on the same side rested on his left hand, brought across his stomach; he squinted as much as humanly possible, but the result was the same:

'No, there's definitely nothing there', he categorically stated, putting his hands behind his back, his right holding the left wrist in an impeccable upright posture, typical of the nobility; even though Gutiérrez was too representing the Catholic Monarchs in the enterprise, Sánchez was far more directly connected to Their Majesties, for which reason the fact he had not seen anything could just as well be interpreted as the Monarchs having not seen anything, either, for such were the ways of the royal court.

'Oddio! I could swear I'd seen it...! Well, no matter; come the morning, after the mist dies down, we can be surer. Still, let the record show, Don Rodrigo, that I was the first to suspect there was indeed light ahead and that the Mayordomo

Columbia: Part I

agreed with me, the both of us overruled only under your watch', Columbus warned the Comptroller, so to speak, therefore quietly making way to the annual pension of ten thousand maravedis for life, one of the journey's upsides the Admiral himself had used several times to keep swaying all other men to his side.

The Comptroller looked at Columbus with a bit of a grin beginning to form on his face, realizing just how petty the request sounded; nevertheless, Sánchez obliged and said:

'The record shall so reflect, Admiral... shall we retire, Gutiérrez?'.

'By all means, Don Rodrigo', the steward told him, slightly bowing in deference to him.

Columbus, being a man with his wits about him, was able to understand that, based on the Comptroller's cheek, he had just been ridiculed in front of another royal official, both probably discussing the subject between them the moment they were out of the Admiral's earshot. Still, he did not mean to claim the reward for himself; it was Beatriz, Diogo, and Fernando he had in mind, picturing the pride on their faces once he told them they were perpetually settled.

He also noticed neither man had addressed him as "Don Cristóbal", as per the Queen's consent when signing the «Capitulaciones de Santa Fé»; come to think of it, it almost seemed they had gone out of their way to avoid it as much as possible during the short conversation. However, they would soon have no choice but to speak to him like an equal.

***

The sailors working around the clock to keep the enterprise operational at the Admiral's request were beginning to yield to their exhaustion, unable to rest not even on Sundays; those whose time was off could not bear sleeping on a wooden floor anymore, missing a regular bed more than anything, except for stability, perhaps, as the constant waving against the vessels, no matter how reduced its intensity was, did not offer comfort at all. Other problems such as trying to grab a wink when directly exposed to either sun or moonlight, the wind, and the occasional tropical storm were equally nightmarish. Sometimes, all that tiredness felt so excessive that the men simply failed to fall asleep because of all the effort it required, an extraordinary event that would never present itself under normal circumstances.

At around two in the morning of Friday, October twelfth, fourteen hundred ninety-two, a mere four hours had passed since the reporting of the Admiral's sighting to both the Comptroller and the Mayordomo, who had already retired to their

Columbia: Part I

quarters in the Santa María's forecastle, as well as both Yáñez and Alonso Pinzón on the Niña and the Pinta, respectively; Francisco Martín, on the other hand, was in charge of piloting the Pinta, but since the flotilla would not be moving any further until dawn, the vessel's shipmaster was fast asleep near the tiller handle with the help of a bit more than just a few drops of mead. It turns out maybe he did not always hold down his liquor after all, but there was no one around to prove it and consequently damn him for getting a hangover.

As for Columbus, he was inside the Admiral's cabin, lying on the only suitable bed worthy of the name in the flotilla. He did not have any more sheets to cover himself with, but there was no need, given the temperature, which was as agreeable as April in Andalusia. Vaguely looking at the ceiling not far above, he was anxious for the Sun to rise behind the trio of ships and cast its rays through the aft windows so that he could confirm whether or not there was actually any substance at all in his claim to having sighted a flame-like light source rising and falling on the wick of a wax candle, both the quietness of the night and the entropy of his thoughts were disrupted by the reverberating cries of a sailor on watch from the Pinta's crow nest, who kept repeating the same word over and over again for every fellow crewman (and the officers, more importantly) to hear:

'Tierra! Tierra! Tierra!'.

The man with the pristine, crystal-clear vision was known as Rodrigo de Triana, despite his having been christened Juan Rodríguez Bermejo (son of Vicente Bermejo, a nobleman himself) twenty-three years earlier. He was the hero of a venture that right from its planning had seemed destined to fail, unapproved of by the most brilliant European minds, and yet, there it was within range, only a grasp away, constituting empirical evidence that it was indeed possible to connect Western Europe to the Far East without spending precious years on horseback, the envoys hoping to make it alive to their destinations, and preferably in one piece, for the dangers of traveling along continental Silk Roads were now exponentially direr than ever before.

Immediately after Triana's first cry, Columbus jumped out the bed, removed the chair holding the cabin door in place (considering the lock had been destroyed), threw it behind him, and ran across the midships to the foredeck on his bare feet. For a moment, it seemed he was about to lose his grip and slip because of the accumulated humidity on deck, but he was fine, breaking through invisible barriers all the way to the forecastle roofing, where he leaned against the taffrail as far as his body would let him, standing on the tip of his toes as he acknowledged the truth. He opened his arms wide,

Columbia: Part I

lifted his chin toward the stars and enthusiastically addressed the Lord:

'Thanks be to God! I've found it! I knew it! I knew it had to be there! At last! Land-ho! Ha-ha!'.

Though Rodrigo de Triana's interjections had been enough to bring most of the crew across the three vessels back from the depths of their sleep, we can assume Columbus' expressions of happiness and fulfillment were the ones chiefly responsible for their effective return to reality.

The officials from all three ships, Captains and masters included (apart from de la Cosa), soon joined the mariners already on deck. Those of blue blood could be seen leaving their quarters in fancy nightgowns with only one functioning eyesight, for the other still had to be duly rubbed and rid of discharge prior to being fully operational again. The nobility question was discarded by Rodrigo Sánchez, the Comptroller, the moment he confirmed Columbus had been right all along, making use of maritime slang as he ogled the reference point from the foredeck stairs in his luxurious robes:

'Well I'll be a seadog's biscuit-eating uncle, Colón…'.

At two in the morning, most naturally, it was quite impossible to fully make out the scenario that lay ahead, just waiting to be freely explored by the newcomers; nevertheless, the irregular pattern in the horizon, omitting and revealing stars according to each man's viewpoint, was indicative of the presence of foliage and canopy, necessarily meaning there was a forest beyond the shore taking up the higher ground. The species of tree was unclear; in fact, it might not even be recognizable to a European, but in just a few hours' time they would all eventually find out.

Having heard the Comptroller, the Admiral turned around and laughed at the comment, adding:

'I told you there was something there, my good Don Rodrigo... I told you!', the Admiral satisfyingly stressed, turning to everybody else across the flotilla and saying, 'Lads! Listen up, all of ye! Sleep as much as you can! Never mind keeping watch, we don't need to be on the lookout for anything else tonight. Try to rest – we make for land in the morning!'.

And having given his new orders, he walked past Sánchez, lifting his eyebrows simultaneously and twice, signaling him not to forget the rightful claim to the royal reward was his. Immediately after, the Admiral remembered one more thing he did not wish to relay in an implicit manner, stepping back and looking the Comptroller straight in his pupils without moving his own, much like a piercing motion:

'Oh!, by the way... you can start calling me

Columbia: Part I

"Don Cristóbal" or "Admiral", for I believe my blood has just turned the same color as yours. It is my understanding we owe it to Her Majesty her will be done right from the start... wouldn't you agree, Don Rodrigo?'.

Unfortunately for Sánchez, he was incapable of restraining his hard swallowing before Columbus walked away; the stern look on the Comptroller's face, together with the twisting of his lips, made it quite clear his reaction had had nothing to do with fear; on the contrary, he was simply displeased at the fact he would soon have to fulfill the Queen's orders and grant the foreigner a nobleman's title, thusly undercutting his own authority in a tad more formality involved than before.

As for Rodrigo de Triana, he was up in his satisfying isolation inside the crow's nest, convinced beyond doubt the ten thousand maravedis a year were his for as long as he lived, for which reason he did not sleep much after the great announcement, simply rendered too excited to grab a wink, let alone forty. He intended to report for duty first thing in the morning, identifying himself before the Comptroller and the Mayordomo as the man to have brought the good news everyone had longed to hear. How it would all go, however, was still quite the mystery. It was likely Sánchez would rather award Triana the sum (considering he was, after all, the son of a nobleman and the nobility is never sufficiently rich) than the Italian meddler, but that was out of the question, as Gutiérrez had too seen the light spotted first-hand by the Admiral and, being the steward to Their Majesties, his loyalty was unshakable. Also, unveiling an inclination toward corruption required a great deal of care and could not be left out in the open just like that for everyone to see; in order to keep secrecy intact between corruptor and corrupted, it was of the utmost importance that the first assess the latter's self-righteousness – especially the lack thereof.

***

Having kept his promise, Columbus came out of his cabin as soon as the Sun seemingly emerged from the depths of the Ocean Sea, just burning through the surface like the star-king it was, and ordered that the sails be unfurled by half for a gentler approach and the caravels' rowboats be prepared swiftly following the drop of anchor.

Dressed in absolute rigor with the best garments money could buy, which he had had especially tailored for the occasion shortly after signing the agreement with the Crown (and well maintained under the care of the Lord of the Wardrobes throughout the entire voyage), the Admiral of the Fleet and of the Ocean Sea, as was his complete title, majestically walked across the Santa María's

Columbia: Part I

quarterdeck and midships section, climbing up the stairs to the foredeck, where the bowsprit pointed straight at the target as if it were saying something like, "this way to Eden". The same cool morning breeze that propelled the sails also made Columbus feel like he was being held and carried on its lap. Had musicians taken part in the ships' company, they could have easily played one of Juan del Enzina's villancicos, namely «Levanta, Pascual, Levanta», composed in honor of the fall of Moorish Granada to the Catholic Monarchs earlier that same year, thus providing the same sort of epic atmosphere Greek theater had once radiated across the hearts of its audience, nearly two millennia prior to this moment.

The general picture was now clearer than ever – the stars seen the night before had gone into hiding behind trees unknown to a lot of these men. Even though they were still relatively far, the shape the bark covering their trunks took made them look like people had sculpted them; some were even bending all the way to the ground, as if they grew horizontally, their canopy crowning them with distinctive foliage – giant blades adorned with others much smaller and thinner, garnished by what appeared to be dark-brown orbs. Their details, however, would have to wait to be scrutinized under a more meticulous observation once the crew went ashore and traversed the dense shrubs blocking the path between trees, leading to the innards of what seemed to be a rather flat lump of land, for no mountain peaks could be seen piercing through the vegetation toward the skies.

As the flotilla approached the beach, though always at a safe enough distance (under penalty of running aground), the water became clearer by the minute, allowing the inspection of the seabed with a naked eye in search for the perfect spot in which to anchor, and that is, as per the most basic rules of seamanship, one where neither rocks nor gravel thrive; not only that, mariners need to be careful not to drift away inland when the lines are a tad longer, preferably bringing the vessel to a stop in a position parallel to the shore, or the undulation will keep pushing it toward an insufficiently deep area for larger ships, which was precisely the case in point.

'Prepare to drop anchor!', the Admiral cried, having assessed the quality of the seabed and its distance to the surface, turning his gaze once more to the landscape, trying to uncover as much as he could.

His instructions were swiftly followed according to the aforementioned procedures on all three ships. All that was left to do at this stage was to drop Jacobs ladders on the side of the vessels in the midships sections, climb down (as opposed to the biblical character's dream, in which he reached the sky as he heeded the Lord's blessings and was surrounded by angels), find a seat in the rowboats and start paddling – the latter was, most naturally, a job for the junior crew.

The Catholic Monarchs' royal standard was held by Columbus himself at the bow, whereas the caravels' Captains, Vicente Yáñez and Martín Alonso Pinzón, bore banners with a green cross in the center, enveloped by the Y of Isabella of Castile and the F of Fernando of Aragon, respectively; both initials were crowned, not only demonstrating who the patrons of the voyage were, but also exerting the couple's right to rule over any and all lands found under the Admiral's leadership, instantly annexing them to the budding Spanish nation, whose laws were applicable in those parts just as much as in Catholic Europe, each kingdom a direct vassal of the Pope and, inherently, God.

As soon as the sea became shallow enough to cover the Admiral's legs up to his knees alone, he leapt from the rowboat that also carried Rodrigo Sánchez, Rodrigo de Escobedo, and Pedro de Gutiérrez, whose presence was essential to officially bear witness to the writing of a new chapter in the History of Mankind, and waded to the beach, whose sand seemed like it had been polished, judging from how it looked so brilliantly whitened. One could say that chunk of land, given its unmistakable purity, was definitely the earthly definition of the biblical Garden of Eden, left untouched for thousands of years ever since Adam and Eve's expulsion, preserved by God up to that very moment, when Humanity was bound to have another chance at redemption, or so were the Admiral's thoughts.

Rodrigo de Triana was also there, manning the Pinta's rowboat, the same that had been partially destroyed after the unnecessary martyrdom of Pedro de Salcedo, though he had two oars at his disposal; the one missing had been found in the orlop in the meantime by none other than Francisco Martín Pinzón, the shipmaster and new pilot, who eventually threw it into the rowboat through the tiller handle gap soon after the purging of most of the rats for what they had done to the vessel's original pilot, thus eliminating any remaining evidence of foul play regarding the man's passing – in short, everyone was covered.

The fresh air of the morning, together with a level of natural cleanliness none of those men had ever witnessed in their entire lives walking on the streets of Europe, heavily polluted with backwater (the perfect source for disease, not to mention the foulest of stenches), was in itself rejuvenating, capable of nursing the exhausted men back to about two-thirds of their former selves, considering fresh food and water were still missing, hence the fraction.

Columbia: Part I

Those who had accompanied Columbus were equally amazed at the sight, keeping quiet to allow the Admiral to savor his achievement. Having taken just a few more steps forward, he chose a spot on the beach and pierced the sand with the royal standard, kneeling immediately after as deference to the King and Queen, though, more importantly, he was bowing to the Lord, saying his prayers for having been spared from a horrific demise that would never allow him to set foot on firm soil again.

Not long after, the Admiral arose and turned back to face the Comptroller, the Secretary of the Fleet, the Mayordomo, and the Captains of the Niña and the Pinta, eventually requesting that they join him:

'Caballeros, if you will please disembark… we have a short ritual to observe before we move along. You too, Captains'.

None of the first three men was too keen on getting his feet and legs wet, but pulling the rowboat up to the beach while they sat in it was impractical, for which reason they had no choice but to comply and just jump into the water. They were carrying between them the manuscript, the quill, and the inkwell necessary to complete the acquisition rite of the land they were the first Europeans to stand on, if not the first people in the world entirely.

'Oh!, come now, Don Rodrigo…!', Columbus exclaimed, 'It's just sand… it'll fall off once you dry up again – don't worry about it', he added, finding the nobleman's obsession with his shoes and hose beyond ridiculous.

'Easy for you to say… they're ruined and not yours', Sánchez retorted, 'but fine – let us move on, then. Don Cristóbal, if you will please read the statement herein…'.

The Comptroller put the piece of parchment he was carrying with him in the hands of Columbus and the latter read it loud enough for everyone present to hear:

'By the grace of the Father, the Son, and the Holy Spirit, and in the name of Their Most Serene Majesties, Queen Isabella of Castile and King Fernando of Aragon, I, Cristóbal Colón, by all the powers vested in me as Great Admiral of the Fleet and the Ocean Sea, Viceroy and Governor-General, hereby claim this land on the twelfth of October of the year of Our Lord fourteen hundred ninety-two and name it…'.

He paused for a moment, trying to come up with a suitable designation, which he eventually found after averting his gaze to the skies and back down again to the manuscript, setting it in stone, so to speak:

'San Salvador'.

Sánchez was about to intervene again when

Columbia: Part I

Columbus finished signing the document, handed it over to the Secretary of the Fleet, looked up to the sky once more, and added, much to everyone's surprise:

'Verbum Domini'.

The others were rendered dumbstruck at the fact the Admiral had completed his assertion of dominance with a reference one would only expect from a priest or any other clergyman. Of the few who understood Latin, the conclusion to the premise was delivered after the men in question looked at each other, shrugging their shoulders ever-so slightly in confusion:

'Deo gratias…'.

Soon after, Vicente Yáñez turned to his brother and whispered:

'I suppose he forgot to add he was a man of the cloth, along with all those titles the King and Queen granted him…'.

Along with a scoff, Martín Alonso nodded in agreement; in turn, Columbus was so focused trying to make contact with the Creator that he did not notice the men's multiple remarks of derision.

Having realized it was probably the right moment to speak up, now that the formalities had been concluded, Rodrigo de Triana approached the Comptroller and asked:

'Sir, when can I expect to be paid the first installment of the reward for being the first to sight land?'.

Sánchez just stood there, his gaze meeting the sailor's without blinking not even once, finally answering with another question after what it seemed like an uncomfortably long time:

'I beg your pardon...?'.

'Well, you see, I was the one who shouted "tierra!" last night and, given the Admiral kept saying throughout the entire journey the first man to sight land would get a reward from Their Majesties, I'm just... making sure you know it was me... sir'.

Columbus had not even heard the mariner prompt the Comptroller, and Sánchez wanted it to stay that way; he had already gone through enough trouble during de la Cosa's short-lived rebellion and most assuredly did not want to deal with another gunpowder-fueled angry man, threatening to explode at any moment and subvert the officers in any possible way he could come up with. Truth be told, nobody had thought de la Cosa had it in him, and yet, trouble eventually found its way, so who was to say this sailor was exempt from trying something crazy of his own? Playing along, Sánchez reassured the young man:

'Of course! Ha-ha! You're the one...! Their Majesties will be happy to commend and present you with the reward themselves when we return, erm...', he hesitated, unaware of what the lad was called.

'Rodrigo de Triana, sir', the mariner completed, figuring out it was his name the Comptroller was after.

'Indeed, my boy, indeed. I will write your name down when we get back to the ship and deliver the news to Their Graces personally', Sánchez told the boy with a sour smile.

Triana thanked him and returned to the rowboat, staying there until further instruction. As for Sánchez, and given Gutiérrez and Escobedo had witnessed the whole episode, he shook his head as a response while averting his gaze from one man to another, for he had no idea what else he could have done. It was a problem needing to be dealt with later, when they returned to Europe, though Sánchez hoped the subject would not arise at all, for the boy was clearly not getting any compensation whatsoever.

Shortly after, Columbus returned with the sword he had forgotten inside the rowboat and, realizing they had been prompted by the young man, asked the three officials:

'Might I ask what the boy wanted from Your Excellencies?'.

'Oh!, you saw that, did you, Don Cristóbal? It was nothing, really... he just wanted to know...', Sánchez replied, seeking for feedback from both Gutiérrez and Escobedo as he shimmied his eyes between them, coming to a stop at the sight of something entirely new lurking behind the trees with the dark-brown orbs on top (which turned out to be coconuts after all, an observation that successfully reassured the Admiral that Asia was in fact close, considering that was the continent they originally hailed from).

'What is it…?', Columbus asked, mirroring the astonished expression Gutiérrez bore on his face, eventually driving his hand to the grip of his sword and looking up to the shingle, where the nobleman's gaze was fixated.

It was then the Admiral realized what had gotten the Comptroller so spooked – they were being observed. Columbus's immediate reaction had had to be the most candid he had experienced thus far in over two months away from home, his mistress, and his children, except, of course, for the multiple times he had felt his blood boiling out of rage and spite; now, a genuinely amazed smile was growing on his face, pointing to his rubicund cheeks.

Chapter VII
Close Encounters of the First Kind

'Dios mío...', the Admiral subconsciously whispered.

Behind the trees whose carved trunks seemed to have been designed by human hands and the dense shrubs in-between, several young men had progressively begun to show themselves, transfixed by the sight of other men whose outlook was nothing short of new to them.

From the Europeans' perspective, the sentiment was definitely the same – the carefully approaching youths were completely nude, just like God had made them at the time of their birth. There were no signs of anyone beyond thirty years of age, and only one woman was accompanying what was likely some sort of either search or hunting party, perhaps. Unlike her male counterparts, she was wearing a cover over her lower privates, possibly made of a cotton-like fabric; the chest, on the other hand, was in plain sight.

Before we move on to the ensuing events, there is a forthright aside we must mandatorily state and imprint onto this piece of parchment, henceforth denying all responsibility for what we may have to report in the near future – for some reason, it is always far easier to notice when a woman behaves differently than expected, unlike the dominant patriarchs; however, and exclusively judging from the viewpoint of these European men (to whom the local youths were a sight never before seen), the usual maritime story applied, meaning that seadogs who had already spent too long aboard a vessel without laying with a woman felt the animalistic urge to take hold of the first they could find and... relieve themselves, shall we say. It is, therefore, no wonder the young woman fell under the leering of most sailors and even some court officials; it always comes down to this, really... the upbringing and the resulting social strata may be astoundingly different from each other, but under the either seemingly respectable coating or the hardened, sunburnt skin lies the one truth – we are all flesh and bone.

It is because of that, precisely, that Columbus

noticed the woman as well, though his thoughts of Beatriz prevented him from entering a lustful trance, gently turning his head back as far as it would go to relay clear instructions to his companions, making use of a soft tone to do so, under penalty of scaring the natives away:

'I will humbly request everyone stop ogling the girl… you're endangering us all with your sinfully pernicious desires…'.

Some of them snapped out of it and cleared their throats, giving it their best to ignore what was common back home only among whores, whereas others turned their backs about three-quarters to make it seem like they were looking at the flotilla, though they were in fact able to continue savoring the young woman with their gaze, almost desperate to get their hands on, have their way with her, and take turns. Whether she realized the white men's intentions was unclear; either way, she came to a stop and let her companions advance in her stead.

Columbus then began to perceive a great deal more details from the local residents – assuming they lived nearby, possibly beyond the natural stockade built by nature; their pigmentation was darker than the Europeans', almost the same tone as the original inhabitants of the Canaries, which was really no surprise as far as the Admiral was concerned, for the Spanish-controlled archipelago lay on the same parallel as this place, so there just had to be some kind of connection between the two peoples. Regarding their hair, not one of them had it fair – on the contrary, it was pitch-black, neatly severed by the eyebrows to uncover their face, but in locks on the back; others even shaved it off the top of their head and had no fringe, letting it grow only from the sides and the back.

Despite their wandering about nude, their bodies, generally handsome and well-built, were ornamented with paint, probably retrieved from plants that grew in the nearby area and produced dyes of their own; judging from the markings on the natives, they either had a preference for, or were limited to black, red, and white.

Some of them bore irregular scars (perhaps a result of violent attacks against them from other natives, wild animals, or even the local flora), whereas others seemed to have been branded according to patterns, each with their own significance. There was also a widespread use of some sort of satchels with a strap around the back and the chest, which Columbus thought was their version of pockets, given the lack of trousers. More importantly, though, only a select few carried a golden ring under their nose, piercing the septum through the nostrils. The Admiral believed maybe seniority might have something to do with it, given the use of this particular ornament was apparently not generalized; it was either that or getting their hands on the source might just be much harder than Columbus thought, something which he did not at all hope for, considering there was a journey to pay for and the land had to be profited from somehow.

Whereas the Europeans were prepared to make use of modern weaponry with the purpose of self-defense, just in case the unpredictable natives decided to attack, the latter, judging from the look of curiosity on their faces, had absolutely no intention of hurting anyone. They were simply wondering, very much like the white men staring at them, who their visitors were and where they had come from.

Columbus was beyond ecstatic, but he knew it would not have been wise to make any sudden moves – not that he feared the youths might do him any harm, but rather that they might flee and make themselves scarce, voiding all chances of developing a friendly relationship with them. The Admiral thus decided to calmly take a few steps forward, going alone in order to make the locals understand he was not relying on a support group that could have, at any moment, shown intentions of seizing them. Yáñez Pinzón decided he should speak up, just so he could make sure what the Admiral was doing:

'Colón... what are you doing...? They might

be dangerous…! Fall back…!'.

Even though the Captain of the Niña had not shouted or made any sudden moves, his prompting of the Admiral had been enough to withhold the progress both Columbus and the natives had collectively completed thus far, forcing the latter to a dubious halt; in turn, the Admiral had to do the same on his end, seeking to undo Yáñez Pinzón's damage by turning his head to the left without looking away from the youths and saying:

'Pinzón, I know what I'm doing. Just stay still and keep quiet. They're not carrying anything lethal, they don't wish to wound me, they're just curious about us. Everybody stand down – now'.

And so they did; the two Pinzón brothers carrying the Catholic Monarchs' banners and the remaining crew took their hands away from both the grips of their swords and the barrels of their harquebuses, making it as clear as possible for the natives they did not mean to use them, even though the youths had never seen anything to the likes of iron blades or firearms in the whole of their lives, no matter how short-lived they had been up until then, for which reason they did not immediately perceive said instruments could damage their physical integrity or even kill them.

Despite the precautions taken under Columbus's command, the natives eventually exchanged gazes between them, as if mustering a mutual

Columbia: Part I

agreement radiating in each other's eyes that the white visitors had come in peace to their territory, instead of posing a serious threat.

Not long after, Columbus had begun to feel nervous, afraid they would all run away because of the Captain's imprudence, but, fortunately for the Admiral, that had not been not the case – one of the natives faced forward and stared at Columbus for a moment, after which he began moving toward him, coming to a stop with only a few inches left between them. Neither man, however, knew what to do next. The Admiral then felt he should go first, despite not having a clue what language they spoke, which is why he gestured, instead of talking, for he believed neither Castilian, nor Ligurian, nor Italian would be much help in the current situation, and that gesture was to lift his right forearm and put his hand out in a greeting manner. The young man did not understand what Columbus meant by it, though he did notice something on the palm of the white man's hand – it was stained with blood, wrapped around by a couple of pieces of dirty and somewhat odorous cloth. Though the Admiral's first intention had been to take the youth's hand and shake it, thus showing him his true colors, only part of his objective was actually fulfilled – the native did grab Columbus's hand indeed, but only to assess it, not shake it. To the Italian, the young man's skin felt extraordinarily soft, perhaps even softer than that of the Spanish noblewomen, despite all the care they took. To the native, however, the Admiral's hand felt brawny, but not in the sense of strength, no – it was calloused and hardened.

Making use of both hands, the native gently untied the fabric wrapped around Columbus's hand, making the latter sigh with slight pain, which did not go unnoticed by the youth, who looked the Admiral in the eyes, realizing how much it must have hurt. The Spaniards were getting twitchier by the moment, and the truth is Columbus's inaction was not helping at all – quite the contrary. Nevertheless, they stayed put. The youth deliberately ignored them, as he was now too focused on the white man's hand's poor condition, and that is why he looked Columbus in his eyes again and drew his attention to the gestures he was about to make, whose message was to keep his hand where it was by firmly holding it, even shaking it slightly, much to Columbus's amazement, even though he knew the greeting stage of the whole interaction was no longer afoot.

The native turned to his satchel, which was hanging from his right thigh, opened the lid with his left hand and used his right to look for something in it. The Admiral could not wait to see what the youth would soon produce. As it turns out, it looked like it was some kind of plant leaf that was

Columbia: Part I

not completely unfamiliar to Columbus or even a few of his men, though the Admiral was not exactly sure where he had seen it or what it was good for; maybe he had read about it in Marco Polo's journals, but what he could tell straight away was that that one leaf was rather fleshy, bearing a few thorns on both sides the native was careful enough not to sting himself with, but there was something missing – he rummaged around in his satchel again looking for a cutting utensil, but apparently he was short of those. He then turned to one of his fellows and spoke.

At this point, Columbus tried to figure out if he had heard their idiom before, possibly in the Canaries or the African coast, given these youths shared a great deal of features with the islands' aboriginal inhabitants prior to Spanish occupation, the Guanches, but no such luck. Though sounds can be next to indescribable, the language these young men used to communicate with each other was, no question about it, sonorously rich. A great deal of utterances seemed quite similar to those used in Castilian and other Romance languages, such as Portuguese and Italian, but codifying them into the Latin alphabet would not have been an easy feat; besides, even if the Europeans did attempt to write the natives' tongue down based on their spelling references, the former could never be sure their transliteration was in fact correct, as the latter most likely used a different set of characters entirely, assuming they wrote at all, which was still an uncertainty.

After a short exchange of words between the young man tending to Columbus and another inside their group, the latter searched his own satchel and revealed what it looked like a fish's tooth, and a big one, at that. Once the native in front of him collected the tooth, the Admiral pointed at first to his own eyes with both the index and middle fingers of his left hand, pointing secondly to the instrument, as if he were asking whether he could examine it a bit more thoroughly. Luckily, the local understood what Columbus had meant, and placed the tooth on the palm of his left hand, but not without warning the Admiral he should be careful when handling it, as it could easily slice through flesh and cause a major bleed, which the native illustrated with his own hands by performing a cutting motion resulting in a hemorrhage as he made a gushing sound and pointed to Columbus's own blood, visible in his wounded palm. Unsure the gesture depicting understanding was a nod, the Admiral went ahead all the same, adding:

'All right'.

The native smiled, waiting for Columbus to inspect the object. It was a tooth indeed, but a rather weird one, and possibly a lot more dangerous than those of exotic animals to the likes of lions, tigers, or any other sort of big felines, considering that, following a warranted closer look, they contained several smaller blades on each side, almost like the iron saws used back in Europe to chop wood, but obviously on a greatly reduced scale in comparison. And just when Europeans thought they had seen everything the world had to show them, nature was yet again proving them wrong.

Having been rendered satisfied with the observation of the sharp instrument, Columbus let it lay on his palm and allowed the native to pick it back up the way he knew was best, so that neither man was rendered injured from that particular interaction. With the tooth back in his possession, the youth began the process of extracting what promised to be a magnificently soothing experience for the Admiral – carefully holding the tooth on the side that had once belonged inside a giant fish's gums and was, therefore, blunt, the native sliced the plant leaf from below and began rotating it as he cut the thorns out, thus obliterating the plant's defenses. Then, he introduced the tip of the tooth under the leaf's upper layer and, having caught a good spot, held it between the tooth and his thumb, pulling it back and peeling it away until the filling that made that piece of vegetation look so fleshy was finally revealed – it was a jelly-like substance, as clear and transparent as the water cresting onto the shore and ebbing away only a few feet in the distance, though it bore remarkable consistency.

Now that the hardest part was done, the native saved the tooth for himself, having put it in his satchel, used his right index and middle fingers as a scoop to retrieve a small amount of the leafy substance, and applied it directly on Columbus's wounded palm in a circling motion. The Admiral's immediate reaction was a bit of an uncomfortable hiss, as it stung a wee bit when in contact with the somewhat necrotic wound, but it soon went away, making him feel immensely relaxed. After he was done with that, the native spoke once more to another one of his friends and asked for what Columbus perceived to be a knotted cotton skein that was applied to his hand in the form of a dressing. In the end, the Admiral was so happy for being treated for both his wound and like a king that he began laughing, bringing everyone else into the giggling, natives and mariners, except maybe for Sánchez, whose expression was of utter nausea – possibly because of the shocking nudity he was being confronted with and that no one apparently felt like doing anything about, but then again, that was his problem, not the locals', considering he was the visitor and his duty was to adapt to the home rules, not change them, though it was in European colonists' blood to always turn things around according to their own desires, no matter where in the world they went.

Before getting to business and asking where one might find the source of those rings in the natives' noses, Columbus had planned to ask for food and drink for himself and his men, simultaneously trying to get to know the local populace better. By means of gesturing, the Admiral pointed to his mouth, pretended to chew, and rubbed his belly as a demonstration of satisfaction after replenishing his strength. Then, he brought his hands together to make a conch and emitted a sipping sound by pursing his lips, showing the youth in front of him he needed to quench his thirst. Finally, he turned around about three-quarters and enveloped his men in a gesture of his arm with the purpose of including everyone in his request for perishables and water.

The Pinzón brothers, the officials, the crewmen, they all stared at both Columbus and the native who stepped forward, hoping the Admiral had made himself clear as far as their needs were concerned. Again, the young man exchanged a few more words with his fellow tribesmen (as the Europeans were willing to call them) and, after having reached an agreement, the frontman gestured they would go get food and freshwater, soon returning to the beach; in turn, Columbus reassured him he and his men would all be waiting for them to come back.

And so they did – the young men and woman went back up the shingle and disappeared beyond the shrubs growing in between the trees. As they walked through it, the vegetation vibrated and produced a leafy ado, soon coming to a stop after being left alone. Shortly after, when the natives were no longer close, the only sounds within earshot were the squawking and screeching of parrots somewhere in the middle of the jungle. No other animals seemed to want to make themselves heard, either because they did not talk much, or because there were not any on that particular chunk of land.

The moment it all went silent, apart from the cresting and ebbing of the sea, Columbus turned around in a swift move and just kept rhetorically talking to his men:

'Can you possibly believe what's just happened?! Dios mío! An entirely different people, a new culture, unknown traditions, walking around nude, never-ending greenage…! Caballeros, I can honestly say Paradise exists outside the Genesis… I mean, I've always believed it was real, but to find it by only crossing the Ocean Sea nearly straight West is just… my goodness me, the very sight of the birth of Man, right before our eyes at first and now underneath our feet… this has got to be the best day of my life…! Someone say something, please! Anything at all! Just don't pinch me! If this is a dream, don't wake me up… or if I'm feverish, then let me die in this trance… now I know God intends to reward me for this discovery when I join Him and the Son in Their Kingdom!', he exclaimed, resembling a soothsaying madman.

'Many congratulations, Don Cristóbal!', Rodrigo de Triana said from the rowboat with a smile on his face, adding, 'I suppose we're both winners. You'll begin to profit from this land soon enough, much to Their Majesties' delight, and I'll collect the reward for finding the source of your riches! How marvelous is that, sir, the both of us being settled for life?', the sailor innocently remarked.

Having heard the inopportune comment right from the start, the Comptroller completely forgot about his ruined hosiery, stared at the mariner, and buried his forehead in the palm of his left hand somewhere around midsentence, wishing Triana could have only had the common sense to keep quiet. As for the Admiral, who had been pacing up and down and even sideways on the beach as if he were in a world of his own (which was true, from a certain point of view), his contentment abandoned him and allowed confusion to take its place, turning to the boy to fire a series of questions:

'What…? What are you talking about, boy…?! Who said you were getting any rewards?!', he asked with a tone of irritation inflaming his spirit.

'I… well, I-I'm just saying that the reward you

kept talking about throughout the whole journey, the ten thousand maravedis for life... I'm the one who's entitled to it, I mean... I was the one who first saw land, and that was the only requirement... is-is it not true...?', the sailor stammered while he made his point.

Columbus's only reaction was to stand where he was, staring at the insolent mariner with flames engulfing his irises; had he had the ability to shoot fire from his eyes, there is no doubt he would have done so without even thinking twice. After an awkward moment of silence whose timing no one could assert for sure, the Admiral stomped all the way to the rowboat, entering the water and splashing everyone in the vicinity:

'Listen to me very carefully, boy – you are entitled to nothing! Do you understand?! You may have shouted "land" before anyone else, including myself, but you were not the first to notice it. It's not that I need to explain myself to you, but I have royally appointed officials who bore witness to my findings! Don Rodrigo! A moment, if you will!'.

The Comptroller was still trying to hide his embarrassment in the palm of his hand, moving in toward his chin in order to cover his mouth and nose, revealing his eyes alone, which he averted to Gutiérrez and then Escobedo, finally meeting Columbus's gaze, who was impatiently waiting for him by the Pinta's rowboat. Being a responsibly

Columbia: Part I

Christian nobleman, Sánchez could swear he was walking in chains toward the stake in the square, not sure whether he wanted to be strangled and then burned lifeless, or burned straight away, which tells us he obviously had no idea what it was like to be sentenced to death and wait for an allegedly purifying fire to slowly boil and consume him as he burst his vocal cords by screaming in excruciating agony. Truth be told, no living person knew what it was like to be engulfed in flames, unless they had previously and miraculously survived such an unspeakable near-death experience; one thing is certain – their lives could never again be the same, rendered permanently scarred and, most likely, in pain.

'Yes, Don Cristóbal…?', Sánchez casually asked the Admiral, pretending he knew nothing of the matter.

'Could I ask you to please explain why this young man seeks to acquire a reward I've already claimed for myself? Didn't you make it clear for the boy I'd seen a light source emanating from this very place yesterday evening, around ten?', Columbus asked the Comptroller, crossing his arms in front of his chest defensively and bearing a rather stern expression on his face.

Before Sánchez could speak, however, Rodrigo de Triana intervened:

'I beg your pardon, sir? You'd already sighted

land before I did?'.

The Admiral turned to the sailor again and said, resting his right elbow and forearm on the rowboat's gunwale:

'Yes, son. I even called the Mayordomo first to help me confirm, and he did indeed see something in the distance. Then, I asked that Don Rodrigo join us, but, according to him, there was nothing in the horizon. It was only after you cried "tierra!" the honorable gentleman realized I was right all along. In short, you're not getting anything – not the ten thousand a year for life, anyway. Plead your case to Their Majesties and ask them if you're entitled to something else for being the first to say it out loud. This conversation ends here. Now, if you'll excuse me, our new friends will probably be on their way by now and I don't want them to be under the impression we're fighting amongst ourselves… that would be the first step for them to realize we're neither orderly, nor capable of subduing them when the time comes. Judging from their simplicity, we've clearly got the higher ground, but we play along for now, ask them politely to take us to their source of gold, and then we see what happens. Either way, both civilization and the One Faith are on our side, so don't mess this up', Columbus explained and confessed, revealing the true nature of his plans to make the natives dance to the sound of his footfall.

Columbia: Part I

While Rodrigo de Triana chose not to continue arguing about the reward, his allegiance to Columbus and Castile in general had been shaken. He did not care what the Admiral did to the natives; it was nothing to do with him. Realizing his prospects of a good life had just been thrown overboard, he rethought his life entirely and knew right from that moment on he would want to follow a different path once they returned to Europe.

As for Sánchez, and even though he was a diplomat whose job was to, therefore, resolve a conflict between parties in a courteous fashion, could not care less about Columbus's intention to make use of the natives; come to think of it, it was actually the best way to exploit the land's natural resources, turning the locals, familiar with the layout, into the Europeans' elite workforce. The same was being done in Africa, so why should the Spaniards fall behind?

Chapter VIII
Los Viajes de Cristóbal Colón

'Your Most Serene Majesties, I hereby present the account of the travels which, by the Grace of God Almighty and the patronage of Your Highnesses, under my command as per your personal and unobjectionable appointment as Great Admiral of the Fleet and the Ocean Sea, Viceroy and Governor-General of the Indies, have established the first ever direct sea route from Europe to the Islands of India beyond the Ganges recently discovered.

'On the eleventh day of October of the year of Our Lord fourteen hundred ninety-two, at around the tenth hour in the evening, as duly notarized by His Excellency Don Rodrigo Sánchez de Segovia, appointed Comptroller of the Westward Expedition to India by Your Graces, I, Don Cristóbal Colón, sighted the Island of San Salvador, where the eighty-nine men and their Great Admiral who originally came aboard said enterprise in Palos de la Frontera, Andalusia, eventually made their landfall, proving henceforth, as God is my witness, the Asian continent is but within a little more than a month's reach of the Canary Islands, constituting yet another domain for the expansion of Your Majesties' glorious empire.

'The Island of San Salvador, thusly christened by myself as gratitude to Our Lord for leading us straight to our objective, never abandoning us or casting us adrift from the path of His eternal light, was originally named «Guanahani» by its native inhabitants, whom I collectively designate "indios", for that is their land, falling under the umbrella of the Great Khan of Catayo, despite their calling themselves "Lucayos" and my readings indicating Cipango cannot be far away.

'During the time I have so far spent exploring San Salvador and the nearby isles, all claimed in the name of Your Majesties, I have come to learn a great many things about the ways of the Lucayo people. They walk about in the nude, exclusively dressing the skin the Lord gave them at birth. They are, in their vast majority, quite young, having not lived a day over thirty-one years of age. Up to now,

Columbia: Part I

I have sighted neither men nor women at an elderly stage of their lives. They are, nevertheless, quite handsome and their bodies exude a level of strength that seems to be innate to them. Without presuming, I can advise Your Majesties as to the benefits of subduing these people, rather by love than by force, most naturally, but, given their ingenuity and lack of modern weaponry, they would never stand a chance against us, should they ever choose to become hostile, which, again, does not seem to be in their nature, much unlike others from the surrounding area, which I believe to be the mainland, where trade most assuredly takes place at a metropolitan scale. The Lucayos are frequently visited by men whose skin tone equals their own, though none of them are as dark as the Canary Islands' natives. Being as friendly as they are, their retribution against the invaders is but a question of self-defense and survival, for they do not wish anyone harm. Their only warfare, if I may name it so, relies on no more than a few bows and arrows whose tips are made of giant fish teeth. Even though their piercing properties muster no comparison to our weapons (for iron cannot be found in these parts, let alone gunpowder), their severing features, on the other hand, are remarkable, almost as if God had intended for them to prosper against any possible threat that came along their way, providing them the simplest means of protection, just as long as they maintain a balanced and healthy relationship with nature, thus coexisting in harmony. Being that iron is something they have never heard of or seen before, it is not so surprising they would try to wield our swords from the blade, innocently injuring themselves.

'Those attacks from third parties are, therefore, the reason for the presence of a few scars across their bodies, mostly concentrated on the limbs and their respective extremities, with the occasional grasp of their chest, abdomen, and back.

'We have come across a few hundreds by now, but they could easily be made slaves and work for us in our quest for gold and spices. That is, in fact, what we have been doing thus far – waiting for them to take us to the source of the ornaments they wear in their ears and noses, which are clearly fashioned from precious metal, and I have no doubt it is mostly gold, even if the inner architecture of said adornments is based on copper.

'I have… recruited about seven men to present Your Majesties with, so they may learn our civilized ways and speak our language, for our attempts to do it the other way around have foundered completely. Without a logical code to the like of our alphabet, it is quite impossible to learn and memorize their vocabulary, but taking advantage of their adoration for us only makes our case stronger. It turns out these poor simpletons will do anything to get our attention, hoping to barter the most assorted items such as cotton skeins, darts, and even parrots for just a few of our glass beads they put on their wrists for bracelets. Others are more attracted to the sound of dangling bells, running all over making the loudest racket.

'Fortunately, whenever we ask for a replenishment of our food and freshwater storages on board, they will promptly bring everything they own to the beach as far as perishables are concerned, much to our satisfaction. Some insist we go ashore, but I make it clear for them I do not intend to disembark, only leading to their approach to us by sea, whether it be in a swim back and forth or aboard what is probably the cleverest creation they may have ever come up with – the «kanoa». To put it quite simply, these are small, yet speedy rowboats directly fashioned from tree trunks. The smoothness of the wood sliding over the surface is admittedly remarkable, and they are made in several sizes, from those only large enough to hold a single man, to those holding up to about fifty, all of which paddle with marvelous synchronization; and should they ever tip over, which I have seen happen during our time here, they promptly make use of the same calabashes they bring us filled with water (except they have to be empty for the operation to be successful) and turn the «kanoa» back into the proper circumstances for their continued travels, not just between isles, but also whenever they wish to reach us, which brings me to what I intended to reveal to Your Majesties earlier on.

'Because of the whiteness of our skin, in high contrast with their natural pigmentation, they firmly believe we have come from the heavens – not that they associate the vocable as we know it to the same promised land of our afterlife in the Lord's Kingdom, no, not exactly… it does not seem to me they worship gods of any kind, though I could still be proven wrong. Either way, they see us as, perhaps, messengers from Paradise, which would make us their guardian angels, in charge of their protection and well-being, something we could definitely provide them with, granted they present us with tribute in order to make them deserving of our constant care.

'According to the indios I chose to bring on board with me, the gold their nose and earrings are made of is the property of a king whose domain is located South of San Salvador, judging from the way they pointed to when asked about their adornments. They say this ruler, as I am given to understand, holds in his possession a cornucopia of gold in its purest form. Before I made my way there, however, I had to mandatorily claim, on behalf of Your Graces, all other islands in the vicinity.

'The first island of which I speak above I named «Santa María de la Concepción», in honor

Columbia: Part I

of Nuestra Señora, Holy Mother of God.

'The second I named «Fernandina», which is my personal homage and unmistakable reverence to His Majesty the King.

'The third I named «Isabella», in unquestionable deference to Her Majesty the Queen. Together, «Fernandina» and «Isabella» constitute a gift of gratitude from myself to Your Majesties for your unconditional support throughout the preparation of this expedition, most wisely sponsored by the insight only Your Graces possess, unlike the rulers of other nations, now sentenced to falling behind as Castile and Aragon make their way into building the largest empire the world has ever seen, surpassing Rome herself – gloria in excelsis!

'It was at this point the indios told me about the city of «Samaot», where the gold of the king of which they speak is mined from. Having decided it was time to make a stop for freshwater, I had a few men disembark and head for the shore on Fernandina. Whether the indios could understand me beyond doubt was unattainable to me – not even my interpreter, Luis de Torres, was able to comfort me during this time of great, personal distress, as he could not gather what they said any more than me. The truth is they could be telling us the most assorted lies just so they could rejoice in our presence, taking us on a wild goose chase. Whether that was the case in point, I will never know, as some of them decided to jump overboard and swim back to their home. My men had it in them to shoot the poor devils and turn them into fish fodder, but I gave the order that they not be harmed. There was no doubt more isles awaited our arrival, as we could see them in the distance, for which reason I was merciful and let them go; I was confident we would soon quench our thirst for gold once we landed in one of them and acquired other indios to guide us down the right path. Besides, if I gave the men who chose to stay aboard the impression we were nothing but bloodthirsty scoundrels, they would never trust us again, failing to convince our future acquaintances to join us or, to say the least, show us the way to the source of the riches they so fondly wore.

'When my crewmen returned, they brought a couple more indios with them, whom I welcomed aboard with great esteem. I asked the sailors for a report on what they had seen, naturally hoping «Samaot», the city of gold, was on the list of their discoveries. As it turns out, luck kept failing to join us; no such urban center had been found. Still, that did not prevent my men from sharing a rather interesting story regarding the indios' day-to-day life.

'The inhabitants of Fernandina were agriculturally savvy, but husbandry was not at all a reality, as they lacked the sort of farm animals (such as cows, oxen, hens, pigs, goats, sheep, mules, asses, horses...) one would be accustomed to find on any other fiefdom in Andalusia.

'What they lacked in agricultural practices, however, they made up for in housekeeping and carpentry (though not masonry). The homes of Fernandina's indios are very well furnished and kept spotless. Their wandering about nude means, therefore, they do not make pigpens out of their household, as one might judge from what would have been a scandalous savagery at the eyes of any Spanish member of the nobility.

'Indeed, their homes resemble booths and their bedding is not set on the floor. As far as I was told and could understand, they resort to cotton nets hung from struts, simply laying there without fear of falling, as it is next to impossible to roll out of these «hámacas», as they call them (my transliteration cannot be confirmed, of course, but this is what the sound they make when they say it suggests would be the possible adaptation to Castilian).

'As for the flora, it too is immensely enriching. The only sorrow I must confess to Your Graces is not being able to recognize any of the trees growing in these parts, for they are abundant in dyes and some of them even possess medical properties I tried myself, when one of our first contacts with the Lucayos helped heal the hand with which I write to Your Majesties; it was not long ago, and yet, my seemingly necrotic palm is now closer to its older self than ever, as if nothing had happened to it, which it did not, honestly, except for some minor friction burns caused by a much too fast running of a line aboard La Gallega.

'Out of this ordeal, one positive thing came – there was a clear agreement between the indios from San Salvador and the ones from Fernandina that Isabella might be our new hope of finding gold, insistent as they were on the existence of this powerful king I deemed to be the Great Khan of Catayo.

'The island I christened after Her Majesty the Queen was a small, delicate piece of land, bearing no mountainous ranges or any other sort of rocky or steep surfaces whatsoever – on the contrary, greenery reigned all over and the fertility of its soil seemed to be quite promising, able to emanate innumerous variants of fruit, both cultivated and wild. I intend to bring with me a few specimens which, hopefully, we will be able to prevent from going bad with the knowledge we are yet to extract from the indios sailing with us, who are most familiar with the conservational processes of which we remain ignorant for the time being.

'Farm animals were inexistent here as well, but there were dogs – and a great deal of them, come to that. Interestingly enough, they were so finely domesticated not one of them barked when they saw us walking among their owners, and they could have easily attacked us, given their massive size – almost as big as lions. Out of curiosity, I wondered what the indios did with these mastiffs, though I was sure I already knew the answer; indeed, they help their owners hunt, behaving quite ferociously when out in the field, becoming remarkably docile and acknowledging of their masters' domain over them once their task is successfully completed. I had yet to find out what sort of wild animals they preyed upon, as none had been sighted up to that point.

'Before leaving Isabella, which I secretly called «La Isla Bella», reminded of Her Majesty's impeccable and immaculate beauty, I also named its westernmost tip «Cabo Hermoso», as was definitely the case, handsomely covered in green, making me all the more believing of a divine intervention in our path across the Ocean Sea, ultimately bringing us to this harmless, innocent paradise, now the property of Your Most Serene Majesties.

'The large island South of San Salvador was our next destination. The indios kept telling me it was an island, all right, but given the extension of its coast, I wondered whether I was looking at Cipango or Catayo; being the latter, we would have finally found the mainland, not just another island, regardless of its size – one the naked eye could not cover in a single blink, not at all. I gathered it might have been bigger than England and Scotland put together, an assumption I felt at ease to make, considering my northbound journeys to both the British Sea and the Northern Ocean about seven years prior to this moment.

'I considered an island this size (or the mainland entirely) had to have several exploiting spots where gold could be mustered from, no matter how friendly the Great Khan could have been to us, offering a great deal of his possessions as a welcoming gift, should he feel the need – depending on his good humor, that is. Of course, still in my possession are the letters of Your Majesties addressed to him, so that we can make peace and enter the sort of negotiations both Your Graces and the Great Khan can profit from immensely.

'Before arriving at the giant island the indios called «Cuba», I sighted one more island to the West and claimed it properly, having named it «La Isla de Arena», not just because of its arid outlook, but also because it was somewhat raggedy, much unlike the previous islands we had already been to.

'Given the indios' insistence on claiming «Cuba» was definitely an island and not terra firme, I chose to rename it «Juana», after Your Majesties' most prized son, Juan, Prince of Asturias. Our landing in Juana took place a little over a fortnight after our arrival in San Salvador, on the twenty-eighth day of October.

Columbia: Part I

'My first impression of this massive chunk of land was how mountainous it was, nearly as much as Sicily. If any of the indios' claims was to be taken seriously, Juana was extraordinarily promising, not only with respect to gold, but also pearls, spices, massive ships, and countless other riches.

'In my attempt at realizing whether they were lying just so they could humor us and avoid any sort of punishment, whether it be physical or emotional (such as denying them entrance in Heaven), I showed the indios aboard La Gallega samples of the spices we were looking for. They told me via gesturing they could undoubtedly be found in «Cuba», constituting just one of the king's many possessions as the ruler of all the encircling islands. As I questioned them a wee bit more about this ruler, I was given to understand he was not the Great Khan after all (known to them as «Cami»), but rather a more local king who, in spite of being entitled to rule his own domain, was at war with a much more powerful lord over the proper definition of borders separating both kingdoms, being that one claimed territories within the other's sphere of government and vice versa, eventually culminating in an ongoing conflict which, much to the indios' despair, troubled their daily routines and way of life in general, fearing for their safety every day. I, however, promised them I would promote a fair dialogue between the two parties, thusly mediating the negotiations with the ultimate goal of achieving peace, for it is our duty as a civilized people who do not require constant involvement in one casus belli after another, as it would unmistakably deplete not only our resources, but turn us into wild animals with a ridiculous need to quench a hypothetical thirst for blood over arguments as petty as who gets which island. Whichever the outcome of my personal endeavor, I was now certain that what was known to them as «Cuba» was in fact Cipango, meaning the Great Khan of Catayo could be found in terra firme somewhere to the West, exactly as Marco Polo described it a scant two centuries ago to Rustichello da Pisa.

'As we approached Juana, I was able to observe its inhabitants were substantially more evolved or prone to labor much harder, to say the least. It is not that their work tools were made of different, or perhaps even sturdier materials like ours, not at all, for I could see the giant blades that grew from the trees we had seen first in San Salvador and were spread all around the area were involved in their fishery process, shrewdly combined with other natural resources such as animal bones (the thought of them being human did cross my mind at some point, but I was willing to reject the assumption entirely, as it would have been far too disturbing, had it turned out to be real).

Columbia: Part I

'We made our way inland through a great river I called «Río San Salvador», bearing in mind the same reasons for which I had eponymously named the first island we arrived at.

'Moving along the coast to the Northwest proved to be a rather fruitful endeavor, for we kept finding several other rivers. I was unsure whether we could sail on all of them, but the indios I kept with me repeatedly told me not to worry, as the riverbeds were deep enough to accommodate the flotilla; considering we had indeed reached Cipango by now, I decided to take their word for it, as they would have likely gotten used to sailing these streams over time with their own majestic vessels, which had me looking for a busy port where I expected trade would be taking place, rendering me eager to find out the sort of goods bought and sold in these parts, not to mention the concepts the indios incorporated into their naval architecture, because, if they were astute enough to produce fast and sleek barges from a trunk alone that could harbor only a few people, then what would their plans be regarding ships especially constructed to travel the seas? I could not wait to feast my eyes on a blissful sight as the one I imagined I would find sooner or later.

'Just so my report to Your Majesties may continue to be thorough, I must let Your Graces know I found an additional three rivers I named «Río del

Sol», «Río de la Luna», and «Río de Mares», respectively.

'We could tell without going ashore Juana's inhabitants erected their homes without giving it much thought as far as urban planning went, given their location bore no architectural logic whatsoever, simply building houses here and there, either too close to each other so much as to endure the nuisance of encroachment, or not at all, almost isolating themselves away from the community. One way or another, the indios of this island also went about naked, unlike the people I could expect to find in Catayo, according to the revelations made by the natives riding with me, who wore clothes covering their entire bodies and not just specific areas.

'About a week had already gone by since the day we reached the shores of Juana, for which reason I eventually decided we should make another stop for the purposes of replenishing our food and water caches.

'Whenever the indios spotted us afar, they immediately retreated, thus making a poor impression of themselves – one rather cowardly, for that matter, and that is why I insist people as feebleminded as these could be easily reined in under control by no more than half our crew; if they do not stand up proudly for their territory, their livelihood, their possessions, then what purpose, I wonder, is there to ceding them autonomy when it comes to them managing their own lives? We are clearly superior in just about everything, something that is not beyond their grasp, given their forthright admiration for us, and must, therefore, weigh in on the actual reason for their presence in this world, which is serving the bigger men. Should they ever resist doing so, then we would have no other choice but to duly punish them for clashing with Your Majesties' authority, commended into Your Graces' spirits by the Lord Himself.

'We came to a definite stop at a natural harbor I called «Puerto de Mares», just off the eponymous river, one day after All Saints'. I can gladly say this might just be the best seaport in the whole world, for it is spacious and the climate here is as delectable as May in Andalusia. I disembarked myself, assessing the circumstances in which a small fortress could be erected on the rocky surface of the newly-named «Cabo de Palmas». I am positive its construction would not only make a fine addition to the assertion of Your Majesties' dominance over Juana, but also prove itself useful in protecting our merchants from hypothetical invasions orchestrated by other, envious nations.

'Having seen the vegetation here was also quite abundant, I asked His Excellency Don Rodrigo Sánchez de Segovia and master-at-arms Diego de Arana they seek for more spices to include in our collection of samples I intend to present to Your Majesties as yet another piece of evidence demonstrating the potential contained in these parts of a new world belonging to Your Graces alone and no one else; along with that task, I also assigned them the royal duty of procuring the king and with him establish loyal friendship as per Your Highnesses request, contained therein the letters both men took with them.

'While we waited for the return of Don Rodrigo and Master Diego, who had gone further inland in the company of one of our indios from San Salvador (thus easing communications between them and the natives by making use of a local interlocutor who was far more familiar with us than the rest), I saw a great deal more specimens of the same medicinal plant whose benefits I had already tested on myself, eventually collecting samples I now also carry aboard with me for Your Majesties' assessment.

'It was not until four days later, on the sixth of November, that Don Rodrigo and Master Diego returned accompanied not only by our indio, but also a dozen others closely following behind, visibly growing fearful as the flotilla came to be within range of their eyesight, which somehow seemed to suggest, as I was beginning to realize, they had never seen ships this big in the horizon, let alone built them. Nevertheless, Don Rodrigo and Master

Columbia: Part I

Diego's account of their grand experience was not empty of fascinating events, which I will now reveal to Your Majesties.

'Having walked about twelve leagues inland (just a little short of forty-two miles, which makes about seventeen hours of continued treading), Don Rodrigo, Master Diego, and the indio arrived at a village of over fifty houses only the day after I had sent them away, during the evening of the third of the month.

'The moment they got there, the natives whose gaze found the two officers' immediately retired to the safety of their booth-like homes, having realized they must have been outsiders, given they were wearing clothes and their skin was fair. The others who were not so attentive soon followed, having realized what the apparatus was all about; consequently, they ended up abandoning the open field, fleeing to the inside of their shelters, where they remained vigilant.

'The only decisive factor that made them cautiously want to come back out again was the presence of another akin to them, who showed no signs of being held against his will or in any physical pain whatsoever, for I always commanded my men the indios not be hurt. I also believe having recommended Don Rodrigo and Master Diego take a native with them was a divinely inspired idea that came to me, otherwise the both of them could have suffered the direst of trials.

'Speaking a language they all understood, apart from the two officials, of course, the indio from San Salvador reassured the villagers they had come in peace, including himself, whose main role was to attest how kind and good-natured the Spanish in general were, the two officials being no more than a small sample of how Your Majesties' people could improve their lives greatly by establishing a systemic relationship capable of bringing all other tribes together under the infallible guidance and wisdom of those the indios thought came from the heavens.

'Indeed, these natives also figured their neighbor had come to them under the protection of two gracious angels who had descended the stairway leading up to Our Lord's realm, only to take back with him as many volunteers as he could, granting them access to the afterlife right there on the spot.

'Even though our little friend from San Salvador swore the other natives had taken him on his word, both Don Rodrigo and Master Diego claimed it had taken a little while for them to leave their homes and reveal themselves completely, their outlook being the same as on all other islands, including the women, who apparently shared the notion that going about with their lower parts out in the open was somehow unacceptable.

'It seems to me (and both Don Rodrigo and

Columbia: Part I

Master Diego agree with me on this) these are quite a hands-on people, feeling the need to touch everyone and everything unknown to them. Fortunately, neither official carried a firearm. The only weapon they could rely on was Master Diego's sword, though, judging from our nearly one-month-old experience living among the natives, the likelihood of having to use the blade was close to zero. Still, Master Diego was wise enough to keep his sword sheathed and secured at all times, just in case the indios felt like taking hold of it and accidentally cut themselves or, far worse, mortally wounded the officials. By this I mean to say the latter were touched and felt, just so the villagers could be sure they were real and not just an optical illusion produced before their eyes on account of the heat.

'Don Rodrigo and Master Diego also told me they were both treated and felt like gods, given the adoration with which they were presented on behalf of the villagers. The flames of their torches highlighted the tone of my men's skin, effectively making them look like heavenly messengers whose wishes the natives were willing to grant as strongly and vehemently as they could, for such was their deference to the envoys.

'They were given food of all sorts, freshwater to drink then and bring back in calabashes (of which we now have a fairly decent collection), and were even shown around the village, having been able to attest the natives' homes were unquestionably sanitary, even though some of them held up to ten people each, or perhaps even more, for both Don Rodrigo and Master Diego figure nearly five hundred men and women, out of a total fifty households, begged them to take them back to Paradise, willing to part with anything the officials asked for in exchange for a ride on our vessels, eventually heading for the horizon, where the sea and the sky unite.

'The truth is, without even having had the chance to ask whether the gold the natives ornamented themselves with or the spices my men carried with them could be found nearby, the latter told me that, at some point, the villagers had run to their homes, swiftly returning to the center of the village, lining up to shower Don Rodrigo and Master Diego with gifts to the likes of, for instance, wooden sculptures of faces (which occurred to me could have been their version of masks, though obviously much different from those found in the Carnevale di Venezia, back in the old country), women (perhaps their depiction of fertility, which is not much of a surprise to a European), and heads whose identity neither my men nor I could assert with absolute confidence, although I am willing to wager they are likely idols, in which case I have no doubt we can easily replace these heresies with crucifixes and other sorts of Christian imagery once we come back, thus relying on the missionary efforts of the clergy, acting in the sole interest of the One Faith.

'This I say with great fervor – if Your Majesties, having the Grace of Our Lord by Your Highnesses' side, overthrew a much more resistant people as are the Moors, I have no doubt these poor heretic devils can be brought into the light so they may clearly realize there is no salvation outside the Roman Catholic Apostolic Church. Once I find a suitable spot for the erection of a small settlement, God willing, a church shall be built there in the near future and the Word of the Lord shall spread from there.

'The last of this tale is, I believe, the most important I have to tell Your Majesties. The moment Don Rodrigo and Master Diego were at last able to inquire about the location of the spices they carried with them, our indio gave them to understand his neighbors spoke of a great island to the Southeast whose size overtakes the whole of the Iberian Peninsula. They also remarked this was a land where men beheaded other men, drank their blood, dismembered them and, finally, ate them like wild animals, which, there being any truth to this story, is a designation applicable to both predator and prey.

'As a sign of gratitude for the information relayed, both Don Rodrigo and Master Diego parted with a few insignificant objects they had taken with them to the likes of glass beads, which the villagers ecstatically accepted as a heavenly gift. Of course, neither of them had enough tokens to distribute across five hundred people, but a lot of them were happy just to be able to touch them, make sure they were made of flesh and bone, just like them, and kiss their hands and feet in deference.

'On their way back, they brought with them several pieces of cotton skeins, which they had seen stored in several homes the night before in their pure form, being that one of them likely held about five hundred arrobas, meaning approximately four thousand quintals can easily be collected each year, greatly advancing the trade of textiles.

'Having been shown a great deal of new herbs, scented flowers, beans different from those we are accustomed to, and corn, the product of an outstandingly fertile soil, Don Rodrigo and Master Diego were also given «cohiba» to try, which is a sort of weed that is introduced in an L-shaped pipe the natives call, as far as I understand, «tabaco»; at this point, the weed is lit, the smoke is pulled into one's throat, held there for a few seconds, and then puffed back out. I have tried it myself and it did feel much too strong the first time, but I gather it only takes growing accustomed to it to make it more pleasant and easier to absorb regarding its medicinal properties.

Columbia: Part I

'As for myself, I waited to see if any of the natives closely following the officials wanted to come aboard, but I suppose fear got the best of them and they fled back inland. Just as well – I was carrying enough with me already and the ship is as crowded as it can get.

'It is now the evening of the twenty-first of November, and we are on our way down the Northern coast of Juana, exploring just a few miles more before we move on to the new mystery island to the Southeast the natives spoke of. As soon as the Lord allows me, I shall continue this account especially conceived for Your Highnesses' pleasure, immortalizing this venture as one of Your Graces' greatest achievements, perhaps even greater than those any other nation dare imagine.

'Praise be to God and Your Most Serene Majesties, Keepers of the Faith'.

Chapter IX
Golden Fever

Only a month away from the winter solstice, nightfall had begun to arrive much sooner, with the Sun setting at around five in the afternoon and disappearing completely close to seven, making room for as many other celestial bodies as the skies could harbor, outshined both literally and figuratively by the star-king and, therefore, incapable of putting a far more pleasant light spectacle together during the day, though this miraculous celestial dome would soon readapt itself to the reality of an absenter golden orb, allowing it to glow no more than ten hours and a half each day for a full trimester.

A great deal of changes had been in the meantime implemented within the flotilla's day-to-day life, much to the crewmen's great pleasure, especially as far as their sleep was concerned, for they did not have to constantly work around the clock on the lookout for land, or worry about keeping the vessels in place overnight, waiting for favorable gusts of wind to return in the morning, having to quickly figure out whether the sails should be furled entirely, just by half, or not at all, while also making sure the ones in use were either enough for the weather at hand, too many, or too few. However, and given the long, hot summer they were experiencing in the end of November, as opposed to the rainy (if not even snowy) winter of Córdoba in particular and Andalusia in general, strong gales were something the sailors needed not worry about, as the environment could not be friendlier, allowing them to comfortably sleep out in the open in the «hámacas» the natives had been offering them for the last few weeks. With the help of the carpenters, everyone grabbed a couple of nails and hammered the tips of each net to certain locations aboard they figured were sturdy enough to hold their weight; using the masts for at least one of the two necessary anchor points eventually became common.

As for the officials inhabiting the forecastles, they too chose to hang their «hámacas» to the walls, instead of lying down on the floor with a couple of blankets underneath to better support their backs; even though they did not use them to cover themselves, given the elevated temperatures, sleeping on them made them sweat all night long, which could turn out to be a nuisance to others when interacting with them (if one did not smell worse than the other, that is, considering bathing was not necessarily a common practice – not even at home), in which case carrying a few pieces of fruit or flowers around could help foul odors fade away.

On a different note, the lack of worries regarding food and freshwater storages also rendered the crewmen a lot happier; they knew if they had to die, it certainly would not be on an empty belly, which is likely one of the worst ways to move on to the afterlife, but if you save a man's stomach, you save his soul just as well. There is, then again, the question of gluttony – a deadly sin, at that, but the sailors did not mind taking advantage of the natives' ingenuity when it came to accepting everything they wanted to offer, as the latter's only explanation for these white men to be walking among them was their divine origin, something none of them admitted to being a lie whenever it came up. It is then safe to assume they were only following the Great Admiral's example, who did not deny the blessing of his aura by God's right hand in front of the locals, either, thus condoning the differentiation between the Europeans' fair skin and the darker tone of the bodies of the people he claimed were "feeble-minded" and required civilizing, somewhat of a euphemism for subduing or, even worse, domestication – this, people's color, had now become the code when sorting out the servants from the masters, just like Europe was getting accustomed to doing with the African slaves that large vessels collected along the continent's West coast – among other merchandise, of course. Powerful African lords were actually the ones stepping forward when dealing with the Europeans, willing to sell their own people in exchange for goods that could only be found to the North, where the whites reigned. Tariffs were paid for these men, subjected to both conversion and christening rituals prior to being swapped in the context of a certain two-way street, from Africans to Europeans as much as the other way around. Not only that, black slaves were much cheaper than the Moors living by the shores of the Mediterranean, as they were easily made Christians and did not attempt to flee at their first opportunity.

In short, and even though the sailors of Columbus's expedition were generally content with these relaxing times, the main purpose of the whole trip had not yet been fulfilled. Up until then, no kings or any other sort of rulers had been found, and no gold mines had been discovered, either, and often because the locals refused to take the Spanish there

– assuming, that is, they could understand each other by means of gesturing, which was not always clear, considering each people had their way of signing something that could mean the complete opposite of what the other sought to signify, unlike eating or drinking, which was quite naturally the same.

Having been through so many islands of all shapes and sizes a little over a month following their landfall in San Salvador, the mariners were beginning to feel, nevertheless, a certain frustration creeping up their spine again, as spending a holiday on the other side of the Ocean Sea, no matter how well-deserved they thought it was, bore its costs, and every day that went by away from home was a day of critical financial losses.

The Catholic Monarchs needed this expedition to turn lucrative if they were to send another in the future, otherwise no one would want to invest in it, regardless of how excellent "a direct westward seaway to India" would sound back in Spain, and the truth is Columbus was well aware of that, for which reason he would have to come up with an idea that would allow him to better secure a spot, perhaps on the island they were headed for to the Southeast, hopefully bearing better prospects than all the others together.

Symbolically, San Salvador was a considerable option, but the island was too small and bore no valuables to justify the building of a settlement there, let alone a seaport to complement it. Aside from this, there was something else worrying the Admiral – so far, the men had been able to keep their trousers up, but every time the local women showed with their male counterparts (to whom they might even be married) to greet the Spanish, a lustful desire made the latter want to take a few of those women for themselves; they were even willing to share them with one another, should they take a fancy to this or that girl in particular. With Columbus around, however, constantly forbidding abusive interactions with the natives some of his men considered were quite normal, such as shooting them and claiming their property (homes, goods and, yes, even the women) without resorting to the much slower and more painful "dialogue and friendship" strategy, it was hard for them to get what they wanted, and if they could not at least have the women while gold made itself scarce, then they might as well go home – enough was enough.

The «indios» aboard the flotilla, on the other hand (and as Columbus called them), were also beginning to emulate the Spaniards' ways of life, seeking to learn the language as best they could in order to make it clear for the Europeans they had been leading righteous lives and were prepared to embrace the heavens, though it was not so easy. Having an interpreter on board, which was the case of Luis de Torres, did not help, either, for neither him, nor anyone else was fluent in the Taíno idiom, as it turned out to be called, also constituting a collective noun for most groups of natives in the area, including the Lucayos.

The natives' outlook was too subjected to a drastic change, as Columbus realized the seamen would not feel too comfortable with other men spread across the deck with their privates showing all the time. As it has certainly become clear by now, had they been women, the Spaniards would obviously not have minded if they took their cotton skirts off; however, being men, the mariners wanted them to wear their loincloths, regardless of the material they used, whether it be cotton or plaited leaves. Still, wishing to conduct an experiment to see how it would go once he presented them to the Catholic Monarchs and their court, the Admiral had the natives try out European clothing, ordering the sailors to part with at least a shirt and a pair of trousers; he had also considered giving them shoes, but knowing they had been walking around on their bare, calloused feet their whole lives, that part of what Columbus deemed to be a more "civilized" outfit was left out, even though the ground and floors back in Andalusia had absolutely nothing to do with the sand and plains the natives were used to – in fact, the risk of injuring themselves on rocks or broken glass while walking on disease-riddled streets, for instance, was immensely elevated and proportional to the risk of having to go through amputation. Should that ever happen, what would the European nobility want with defective pieces of merchandise such as those? Owning slaves was supposed to ease the burden of one being white by having an inferior take care of oneself, not one taking care of another. Much to Columbus's disappointment, however, the natives insisted on removing the clothing, as it made them feel simultaneously hot and entrapped. Little did they know that was but the most harmless tip of what entrapment could feel like.

* * *

While the Admiral produced his account of the journey up to that moment, working on it compulsively lest he forget about the smallest details, Martín Alonso Pinzón, Captain of the Pinta, was restarting to lose his patience with Columbus, much unlike his brother Vicente Yáñez, Captain of the Niña, who had inclusively been the first to question the Admiral about the extra two hundred and fifty leagues the latter had been seeking to conceal from the sailors' knowledge in the beginning of October.

Indeed, approximately a month and a half and well over four hundred and fifty square leagues of land and sea area covered later, Martín Alonso

Columbia: Part I

made the decision, together with his crew, to abandon not just the Admiral, but also his brother Vicente Yáñez, keeping in his company the middle one alone, Francisco Martín, who, as pilot of the Pinta, had no choice but to go along, even if he thought otherwise:

'I don't know, Martín… after all this time we've been together and the episode you were involved in with Colón and Vicente…', Francisco Martín reluctantly told his brother while they conversed at the table inside the vessel's forecastle, adding, 'if the man hadn't pushed his servant's loyalty to him, we would've probably starved, found a typhoon and become fish fodder scattered all over the Ocean Sea, by now. For God's sake, we can't keep backstabbing each other the first moment something doesn't hail our way…!'.

'You know perfectly well this isn't the first moment something hasn't hailed our way, Paco', Martín Alonso began to say, rising from the table and adding, 'these indios have been taking us for a ride the whole time! If we stick to Colón's plan of fake amicability toward them, we'll never find any gold or spices to sell and the money we sank on this expedition may as well have been cast into the sea. I mean, you can count, Paco… our savings are gone, we're not profiting here, we're not profiting back home… how long do you think Colón or any of us can keep this up? He's become desperate, brother, believe me. It's like he's willing to go around the world until he finds a damned gold nugget, just so he can hurry back to Palos and tell the Queen there are mounds waiting to be mined! And what of all the spices, Paco? Where are these famous spices that were supposed to make us rich? We had to pay the Portuguese for the samples we brought, did you know that? And what did we do with them? We showed them to the indios, they said they grew all around. We let them taste them to make sure they were the right ones, they kept pointing here and there, babbling in that weird language of theirs a great king had everything we were looking for, and where was that king…? Nowhere!'.

Francisco Martín understood his big brother's frustration, but he kept trying to cheer him up all the same:

'Fine, I admit the natives have been probably making fools out of us, but we haven't covered that great an area… most of the islands we've been to are small, sandy… we haven't even spotted a single mountain. Gold isn't just going to jump out of the ground and fall into our raggedy bags… we need to find a big rock and turn it to dust until those glowing pebbles are all that's left'.

'Aye, Paco! Exactly!', Martín Alonso exclaimed, 'And that's why we need to grow a pair, leave Colón behind and start exploring ourselves before he gets there! Look… I've told you, Paco –

Columbia: Part I

these people scribbled all over have no intention of showing us where they keep their booty, that much is clear. They try to make themselves look gullible and fragile with all the nudity, but I'll bet you they're much smarter than they let on. All that royal nonsense about handing over the King and Queen's letters to the "Great Khan"… what is that…?! There is no "Great Khan", Paco – not in these parts, anyway. Colón thinks he's the only one with brains out of all of us, but he's not. I've heard about his idol before, Marco Polo. I know about his expedition via land and let me tell you – what he saw has nothing, absolutely nothing to do with what we've seen up to now. Everything is different… the climate, the trees, the bushes, the fruit, the ground, the animals, but most importantly, Paco, most importantly, none of what these people do or look like is in Polo's journal – nothing. If we wait any longer to be taken God knows where, hoping to find the ruler the indios are going to come up with next, we're done for. The men agree with me. Do you?'.

Francisco Martín remained silent for a moment, his elbows resting on the table, his fingers intertwined and his lips pursed, looking into the void, trying to come up with a better option than breaking apart from the flotilla.

'What does Vicente think?', he asked.

Martín Alonso inhaled deeply, crossed his

arms in front of his chest and said, initially averting his middle brother's gaze:

'Whatever we collect, we split with him. He's our blood, so we're obviously not going to leave him out of this… and that's why the moment we do find something, we go looking for him, we bring Colón along, and we do it like men of honor – we share. But for now, we tread our own trail. I don't trust these nudes, Paco, I just don't'.

'So, he doesn't know…', Francisco Martín asserted with a stern expression, waiting for Martín Alonso to look him in his eyes.

'No… no, he doesn't know. I haven't had the time to talk to him alone. We haven't been going ashore, boarding each other's ships is too suspicious… plus, Colón is always watching like a bird of prey, making sure no Spaniards pull his leg, when it's the indios he should watch out for', the eldest Pinzón brother confessed.

'Very well…', Francisco Martín said, loudly exhaling through his nose as he ogled the table's surface, breathing back in again and looking at Martín Alonso once more to ask:

'What of Quintero and Rascón? Are they with you this time, or do they feel like breaking the rudder again so they can stay with Colón?'.

'They're in; everyone is. The one person whose answer I'm still waiting for is my pilot', Martín Alonso replied, leaning in on the table to support his weight with the palm of his right hand and placing his left on the side of the waist, waiting for his brother's decision.

After meeting Martín Alonso's gaze for a few moments, Francisco Martín said at last:

'So be it'.

He got up and the brothers held and patted each other on the back as the co-owners of the Pinta entered the forecastle. Gómez Rascón was still wearing a cast because of Martín Pinzón's accidental harquebus shot to his arm, but the medicinal plants retrieved across the several islands, combined with a rather odorous mixture of animal fat, egg whites, and flour from the journey's original food caches, seemed to be healing his limb up nicely. He could not wait to get rid of that solidified foul-smelling concoction, and neither could the others standing close to him. Cristóbal Quintero, however, was the one whose turn was to speak:

'So? Are we ready?'.

'Colón's put his lamp out at last. He'll soon be asleep', Gómez Rascón added.

Alonso Pinzón turned to both men, then his brother, seeking confirmation once more through his eyes, and back to the vessel's proprietors, saying:

'We're ready. Let's do this'.

On deck, the men awaited the Captain's order

to drop sail and move along to where Columbus intended to go next, without waiting for the slow effects of diplomacy. Martín Pinzón, in turn, climbed the stairs down to the orlop, untied the lines holding the tiller handle in place and turned it gently to port, coming about once the sails were in place, slowly lowered to reduce the noise to an absolute minimum. Little by little, a cresting and an ebbing at a time, the Pinta disappeared without a single lamp on and into the dark, leaving the rest of the flotilla, La Gallega and the Niña, all by themselves while moored at Puerto Príncipe, just below Río San Salvador.

***

At dawn, the Admiral was getting ready to start a new day of exploring still inside his cabin, when Pedro de Terreros knocked on the door:

'Almirante? It's Terreros'.

'Come in', Columbus said as he buckled his scabbard around his waist, sheathed his sword, and put on his hat.

Terreros opened the door, fixed in the meantime by Antonio de Cuéllar (the carpenter) to the best of his abilities, though the patch was not too brilliant, mainly due to the lack of proper tools and resources, and closed it behind him as he said:

'Good morrow, sir'.

Columbia: Part I

'Is my breakfast ready, boy?', Columbus asked him without facing him.

'Aye, sir… how-however…', Terreros stammered, drawing the Admiral's attention to him.

'What?'.

'Well, sir… it's about… la Pinta, sir', the boy told him, nervously rubbing his hands together.

'Oddio, did those two idiots break the rudder again? First, they don't want to come. Now, they want to overstay their welcome. Every day a new problem, cavolo! Quinteros! Rascón!', Columbus shouted, heading for the broken window to see what had happened, lowering his voice after having realized something was off, 'Che cosa…? Wasn't she on our portside? Where has she gone…?'.

Terreros then felt he should further explain the purpose of his visiting the Admiral's quarters first thing in the morning without bringing breakfast:

'That's wh-what I came here to tell you about, sir…'.

'Tell me what?! Go on, boy! Speak!', the Admiral told Terreros, forcing him to spill the beans.

'La Pinta is nowhere in sight, sir. Don Rodrigo, Mayordomo Gutiérrez, and Secretary Escobedo believe she may have left during the night, but they've no idea where', the boy said in only one draw of breath, having inhaled deeply once he finished.

Columbus stood by the window, staring at Terreros with a red-hot piercing gaze, as if a blacksmith were forging swords inside his irises; it almost looked like he had become a raging bull. In turn, the boy knew not where to avert his sight, where to put his hands, or what to say, seriously pondering making a run for it just to avoid the blazing iron in the Admiral's eyes, but the latter was faster than him and took the first step. Terreros could swear Columbus was about to have a go at and throw him overboard, but, instead, he turned to the door just inches away from him, opened it and left on a quick pace. The cabin's boy closed his eyes and sighed silently, though profusely and with tremendous relief.

Outside, on the quarterdeck, the three officials were waiting for Columbus to come out and reinforce the news he had just heard. Sánchez, the Comptroller, was the one to speak first:

'Ah!, there you are, Don Cristóbal. Has the boy told you that…', but the nobleman failed to continue, for the Admiral walked past him and the others at an incredible speed, immediately heading for the portside stairs leading up to the poop deck in order to confirm the Pinta had in fact vamoosed, which she had.

Without wasting another second, Columbus walked across the poop deck to the starboard side and cried out:

Columbia: Part I

'PINZÓN! PINZÓN, GET OUT HERE! GET OUT HERE NOW!'.

A few seconds later, Vicente Yáñez, the Captain of the Niña, opened the forecastle door and came out running across the midships with his proverbials down, not having had the time to finish his morning business properly, thinking an emergency had erupted and his presence was instantly required. The crew of the Santa María had already noticed the disappearance of the Pinta, along with a few men from the Niña, which was always further away from the former, given Columbus's insistence on keeping the flagship in the center (perhaps to prevent the Pinzón brothers from communicating without his knowledge), thus leading to a slight negligence on the Niña's crew's part.

'Coming! I'm coming! What is it, Almirante?! Has something bad happened…?!', Yáñez Pinzón asked as he climbed the stairs to his vessel's poop deck, nearly tripping for pulling his trousers up a tad too late.

'Where's your brother, Pinzón?! Where has he gone?! Where did he take the Pinta?! Why was it moored next to my ship just a few hours ago and now it's not?!', Columbus fired at the Niña's Captain ever-so intensely that not a sound fell into the void between La Gallega and the Niña, thus preventing the surface of the Ocean Sea from absorbing any syllable whatsoever.

Even though Yáñez Pinzón had understood the contents of the Admiral's enraged utterances, he failed to realize what Columbus was talking about. It was only after he sought a better spot to position himself and look beyond the Santa María that the Captain perceived at last what the Admiral had meant, though his response was, as we know, not as informed as Columbus was sure it would be:

'I... I have no idea... as you said, it was indeed by your portside, but... it's not there, anymore...'.

'Wait... wait, wait, wait, wait, wait...', the Admiral emphasized, positive that Yáñez Pinzón was in on the ruse and was trying to make a fool out of him, 'you mean to tell me you don't know where the highest-ranking officers of the Pinta, who happen to be your brothers, have taken the vessel...? Is that what you're telling me? That the three of you could never have considered plotting against me? It wouldn't be the first time, now would it, Pinzón?!'.

The Captain of the Niña's feelings of incredulity and confusion were now progressively yielding their places on the podium to a sense of betrayal and rage, the latter directed not only at his brothers, but also Columbus, given his unfounded accusations:

'I don't care who appointed you Admiral, Viceroy, Governor, and whatever the hell else you call yourself, Colón, even if it had been the Pope himself! I will not have you talk to me in that tone! This may come as a surprise to you, but I am as dumbfounded as you after realizing my own brothers ran out on me! You might feel insulted, but the damage they've done as far as I am concerned is much greater, and you know why?! Because they're my kin and it hurts me to see they've left me behind! Whatever it is they're up to, I'm not a part of it. Another classic case of the youngest sibling being left behind…! Are they out looking for gold?! Have they left for Andalusia to be the first to break the news to the King and Queen?! I don't know! What I do know is you should bite your tongue when accusing me of being a part of any "plots", especially a desertion! Have you already forgotten what we've both been through?! We were caged like animals…! For God's sake, a young boy was murdered trying to rescue us! All this time I've stayed by your side, supporting your every whim! How dare you accuse me?! I've nothing to do with this, but I will leave you like they've left us if you don't knock it off!'.

Even though Yáñez Pinzón's retort continued beyond the point where he asked himself whether his brothers could have sailed away back to Spain to be the first to tell the Catholic Monarchs about the expedition's results, Columbus failed to absorb any further information, having become inert at the thought he could lose his rights to all the land found in the area, their people, their properties, and, most importantly, the revenue he planned to obtain from future settlements where hypothetical members of the Castilian nobility might intend to invest (the previously agreed upon ten percent, as per the terms of the «Capitulaciones de Santa Fé»).

Feeling overwhelmed by all these ghosts creeping up his spine and into his brain, forcing his imagination to run wild, Columbus looked like he was about to fall into the abyss, his eyes wide open and dry from a lack of much needed blinking. His hearing had also become impaired, or so it seemed for a while, until he finally heard Yáñez Pinzón repeatedly calling him:

'Colón! Colón! Wake up, Colón!'.

The Admiral eventually did wake up from the trance and noticed the crewmen of both vessels were looking at him, including the officials he had ignored on his way to the poop deck and the natives lying on their «hámacas» with their necks up; the latter could not understand the exchange of words between the two white men, but they could obviously tell something wrong was afoot.

Rubbing his lips with the tip of the fingers and the palm of his right hand, now duly healed after the regularly applied «aloe», as he had found out was called, Columbus cleared his throat, sore from all the yelling, faced Yáñez Pinzón (without looking him in the eye) and said, loudly but calmly:

Columbia: Part I

'You're right, Pinzón. I apologize for channeling my anger at you, even though you clearly did nothing I should blame you for. Your being here shows me how loyal you are to me, and I appreciate it deeply… ahem', he finished, looking down again as he put his hands behind his back and balanced his weight from his toes to his heels and vice versa.

Remaining silent for a moment, the Captain of the Niña nodded gently and calmly replied:

'Thank you, Colón. I'm glad you see it the way I do'.

'Well… "don't look a gift horse in the mouth", so people say'.

Yáñez Pinzón was somewhat unsure whether he should take the adage for a compliment or feel offended by it, but the Admiral's apologies, which had seemed honest, prevented him from walking down the conflict path yet again, as they were all tired in general and felt beyond exhausted every time they argued.

'Now… considering I have everyone's attention', Columbus ironically remarked, given every man from both La Gallega and the Pinta was looking at him, 'prepare to raise anchor and set sail; we're leaving for the new island to the Southeast. Man your stations!'.

And so they did without questioning the Admiral, encouraged by Yáñez Pinzón's nods, which he did without letting Columbus see them – his pride was already hurt enough as it was.

Chapter X
Ayiti

'It was shortly after Boinayel returned to his cave to rest from his daily stride across the skies and allowed Marohu to come out and begin his nightly watch that we saw them for the first time ever, probably since the beginning of the world, as created by Atabey and her twin sons, Yúkahu and Yuka; those of whom I speak are men, different from any others to have walked among us or through our plains, descending from a lineage of which Lokuo had clearly not been the founder, for they were white as bones, covered in almost their entirety by pieces of cloth varying between them all, hued with several shades – some darker, resembling our bodies, and some clearer, nearly as pale as their faces and the palms of our hands. About three or four of them wore flame-tainted garments, as red as the dye used to paint our visages. I could honestly say the tone of their skin was a near reflection of Marohu's pearlescent radiation.

'These men had come to us in two out-of-proportion wooden barges, none of which looked like our kanoa, not even the largest, the sort we could fill with up to one hundred and fifty of us, even though they were much less (probably about fifty) and rode those giant water sliders, anyway; the latter bore several thick poles pointing toward the heavens, except the foremost, which looked like an arrow aiming for land, each of them ornated with big panes of cotton blown by the winds, though I cannot be sure of the material. In the distance, we saw them cast a couple of double-edged hooks into the waters, seemingly holding their insurmountable constructions in place. Each barge carried a smaller craft tied to the back by a thick vine, and that is what they used to come closer, rowing their way through Yuka's aquatic domain, though only one, perhaps two men, depending on the craft, used paddles somewhat similar to ours, simultaneously pushing the water out of their way as they kept moving with their backs turned on the shore, except for the all other occupants, who had by then perceived we awaited their arrival on the beach. They carried with them a few black receptacles containing dancing flames guiding them along their path as they rowed toward us.

'Up front, one man, who was carrying the same sort of illuminating contraption and I suspected was the others' leader judging from his posture, brought with him a pole from which a pane covered in symbols hung. I gathered they had a visual system they used to record events and make certain statements, very much like ours, only their inscriptions were fused into the cloth itself, instead of drawn on sturdier surfaces like the rock walls we were used to in the caves, not to mention their selection of hues seemed to be far richer, bearing a few colors we could find all around us, though not reproduce. Their shapes looked odd, as well. Two other men riding on the other craft also carried poles with panes different from and smaller than their leader's, which was probably a way of asserting his dominance over his servants.

'When they reached the shore at last, they jumped out of their crafts and into the water, striding up the beach about halfway from the spot my people and I had been observing them with the help of our torches covered in sap. As per our custom, I stepped forward and introduced myself, welcoming them to the land of our forefathers, saying, "Welcome, White Travelers. I am Guacanagaríx, Cacique of Marién. These are my fellow nitaíno. You would do me great honor if you accepted my invitation to join us in our village and eat with us, so that you may share the tales of your origins and the reasons behind your coming here". For some reason, the leader seemed to have taken a fancy to my guanín, ogling it like he was in some sort of a trance, his eyes absorbing its glow like life itself.

'A few moments later, I noticed a couple of our kin were among the whites. My warriors, immediately thinking they were being held captive by the outsiders, drew their bows and arrows laced with poison and aimed them at who they thought were either captors sent by the Kalinago under the guise of men painted with the color of the dead, or the Kalinago themselves, living in the isles on the outer rim. Either way, contact had had to be made in order for these people to come to our island, traveling aboard those enormous barges and covered with tailored fabric from head to toe.

'In turn, the whites' response was to point back at us some sort of thick, hollowed sticks of considerable length requiring the use of both their hands to keep them steady. Wherever I looked, I did not spot any arrowheads or other kinds of warfare they would have been able to shoot at us. I could only assume it was all but a ruse to make us stand where we were, even though nothing could have happened to us – unless they threw their sticks in our direction, of course, but the snag was they would have lain on the ground before hitting anyone, pierced by an arrow that would kill them soon after by thickening and engorging their blood, should the tip fail to do so straight away. Others, however, were wielding objects that reacted to nightlight, shining from different angles. Those among my men who had not drawn their bows responded by wielding a macana each.

'Regardless, what was important was that nobody put the lives of our two naboria friends at risk, a problem they eventually solved all on their own when they spoke up and told us the white men were actually their cohorts, having treated them nicely since their very first encounter in Guanahani not long before. They said the ail-looking men had come from the sky to take them to Paradise aboard the great barges and that, aside from that, they were looking for the mines where the source of our ornamental rings and my pendant could be found, as they were only willing to make a trade, capable of producing several items that would give us great pleasure to possess in exchange for a few pieces of said source. The naboria mentioned also they called themselves "Krishtianosh" and intended to spread their beliefs in a single zemí they called "Diosh" (creator of the skies, the earth, the sea, responsible for the splitting of light and darkness, maker of men, both them and us – which I found somewhat distasteful), together with his son, who were one and the same, complemented by a third entity they called "Eshpíritu Santu", revealing of the presence of the former two, and whose representation they did not fashion out of any materials whatsoever, apart from someone they called "Hezúsh", their lord and savior, killed by their ancestors to atone the sins of every man to have ever walked the land and those yet to come. I was given to understand "Hezúsh" was the son of this "Diosh", who were, then again, one and the same, but of that I remain unsure.

'Although I had been rendered interested in the account of our neighbors on our visitors, I was quite certain it must have all been no more than just a tale very few of us would even care to listen to, as it made little to no sense. Still, we were aiming weapons at each other and the tension needed to be defused, so I gave my nitaíno the order to stand down. The leader of the whites, apparently choosing to walk a path toward friendship, must have mirrored my words in their language, one I could tell involved a great deal of tongue, as the tip kept leaping in between his jaws like a hurdle... I even wondered if it could have been a form of exercising this bodily aid we all had in common and was required for our utterances to be perceptible. One way or another, his fellow sickly-looking allies obeyed him, putting an end to the verge of unnecessary violence. The man in question then slowly approached and showed me the palm of his right hand. I knew not what he meant by it, but the best I could think of was to show him mine and let him decide what to do next. He grabbed it gently, which eventually unnerved my warriors, but I told them yet again to hold still. Soon after, he took his left hand and bent my fingers around the one I was touching, having us both hold each other's palms. He made an up-and-down motion twice and smiled. The naboria intervened and said it was their way of greeting one another. Finally convinced they meant us no harm, I smiled as well and shook his palm vehemently, which seemed to amuse him and the others. His skin in this particular area of his physique was so soft that I believed he had somehow been in contact with aloe. I could tell our neighbors from the North were already somewhat familiar with the customs of the whites and asked them to keep close, just so they could explain what was going on every time our visitors chose to interact.

'We reached our yucayeque around supper, when Marohu came to be directly above us, halfway in his crossing of the sky, walking the long road every day back to his cave, soon after allowing Boinayel to take his place in what we all hoped would be an endless cycle.

'Needless to say our company attracted a great deal of attention the moment we approached and moved toward the batey. My presence and that of my nitaínos reassured the people it was safe for them to come closer and take a better look at the frail-looking men. It then came to me that that was likely the reason for their choice to wear several pieces of cloth all at once, including the covers on their feet, considerably rigid and tightened by fancy strings. I gathered it must have been rather uncomfortable to conceal their extremities in such a manner, but... those may have just been the parts of their bodies they prized the most, considering they got all that care and attention.

'And just as my people had become ecstatic with the newcomers, so had the latter's attention been drawn to the former – the women, especially, and not just because of their jewelry. We have a rule concerning attire based on marital status – men and women who are already married conceal their parts, but those yet to wed wander as they were born. Our visitors, however, seemed to make no distinction between them, as they did not care enough to realize when they were staring, lustily tasting our wives, daughters, and sisters with their gaze. Their leader, with whom I intended to converse during supper, seemed to admonish a lot of them, but as soon as he turned his back, they leered all over again. To the thirsty men's great disappointment, however, both girls and women retired to their exclusive area of the yucayeque (where they were in charge of themselves), the men and the boys being the only ones to stay behind (should the latter be old enough not to require their mother's constant attention).

'Having nowhere else to ogle, I deemed the whites ready to eat and satisfy themselves properly with the best food we had in store, so we sat in an elongated ring in the batey, thus allowing everyone to see each other and engage in conversation whenever and wherever. Even though they were guests, at least their leader required I offer him a seat between myself and the bohique in a duho like ours, which pleased him immensely; all others helped themselves to the ground, which I could see from their body language it was something they were not used to doing.

'First, we made the usual bread offerings to our zemís. Then, as I collected my share and split it with the leader of the pale-looking in a demonstration of amicability, everyone else was welcome to take their part. Before we could advance, however, we prized our visitors with music, singing, and dancing at the sound of the maracas, which they greatly appreciated.

'The feast we offered was sufficiently varied for spirit-colored folk to pick whatever they liked best. Our meat delicacies ranged from iguanas to birds, turtles, worms, hutias, waterfowls, and others. Remoras, mussels, and oysters were what the waters yielded from their bed. Any of these could be garnished with what the hand of Atabey made emerge from the ground, like yuca and batata, along with mahíz. All this I explained to our guest of honor, whose name I memorized as "Koló".

'Our conducting of business eventually led him to ask about our land – how big it was, were there many of us, where could the source for our jewelry be located, did we have any enemies, who did we worship, and several other questions the Guanahani naboria helped me interpret, doing the same for him as I revealed everything he wished to know. I told him there were different Cacicazgos across the island, each strictly defined by natural borders and governed by a Cacique; at that moment, they were in the Cacicazgo of Marién, of which I am the ruler. I could not precise how many of us were there, but I did tell him we were as large in number as him and his group replicated indefinitely. As for enemies, we often needed to watch out for attacks, not just from the Kalinago, but others living much, much closer to us, such as Caonabo, Cacique of Maguana, located in the center. Koló asked me if he was the one who usually tore his enemies apart, ate their flesh, and drank their blood from their skulls, keeping their bones for spoils. I confirmed Caonabo was indeed quite aggressive and ferocious, having traveled from the land of the Lucayos to the center of ours long ago, eventually garnering a great deal of admiration because of all his

Columbia: Part I

knowledge and aptitude when it came to fighting and war in general, commending enough respect to be chosen as the one true leader, but he did not eat anyone's flesh, nor did he drink their blood; I imagined Koló must have mistaken Caonabo for the Kalinago, similar in sound, which was understandable.

'Regarding our religion, I asked the bohique tell him about the origins of the world, which he did, beginning with Atabey, her twins, and her other self, Guabancex, responsible for the disasters we should all endure whenever when we failed to please our ancestors. Though she was Atabey's counterpart within herself, she too had had twins – Guataubá and Coatrisquie, zemís of juracánes and floods, respectively. Other primordial zemís included Boinayel and Marohu; they were also twins, sons of Iguanaboína, who brought us rain every time our crops' thirst needed quenching and clear skies once they were satiated. They grew with the aid of Baibrama and Yuca himself. The ruler of the dead was Maketaori Guayaba, and his domain was called Coabey, kept under strict watch by Opiyelguabirán, whose head as that of a dog. Here, Koló remarked he had once heard about a similar creature back where he hailed from, except his was three-headed and could only see with his eyes shut, much to our amazement. He quickly added, however, it was no more than a story no one believed in anymore back where he came from, as men and women had been shown the light and glory of "Hezúsh", their ultimate lord.

'Deminán Caracaracol, idolized as a zemí just as well, had been the first man to set foot on the earth and was considered by us as a hero. Macocael, who should have watched over the domain of men, ended up turned to stone as punishment. "Adán", Koló mentioned, was what the people in his land called who they thought was the real first man to have walked the earth, thus descending from his union with "Eba", the first woman.

'As delighted as we might have all been with these stories, Koló's persistence in constantly repeating the names and people he mentioned were the only important ones had begun to irk not just myself, but the bohique and the nitaínos in general. It had been disrespectful of him, to say the least, to imply we were wrong and had always been regarding our spirituality; even though he never said it outright (according to the naboria, anyway), we were all sure he was dying to.

'Seeking to avoid confrontation after an agreeable meal, which would have been a terrible waste to both sides, I diverged the conversation to his interest in the source of our jewelry and spices as we offered tabaco, something the whites apparently knew about, though their ability to hold down the smoke and savor it required some tweaking, as we

Columbia: Part I

could easily perceive from their coughing again and again.

'Koló eventually revealed he required proof of the existence of seasoning and what he called "oro" in our land, so he could return to his masters and please them with said offerings. Now that was something we could relate to, as all of us had tasks to fulfill for the benefit of the entire Cacicazgo in general and each yucayeque in particular. I replied we would all choose a tribute from our bohíos as a token of our friendship toward this group of whites and everyone else waiting for their return, so that we remain close companions and allies, always willing to welcome them back or anyone new for a memorable first time – for this Koló said he would forever be grateful to me and my people, rendering us as happy as they were.

'Objects to the like of masks, talismans, stone and wooden zemí sculptures, necklaces, rings, full-grown seasoning plants, seeds, yuca, mahíz, batatas, cotton tunics and belts, shells, calabashes, and maracas were only a few of the presents we wished the white men would take back to their barges and their homeland with our greatest esteem. I should note, nevertheless, not all of them looked as happy as Koló about their new possessions. For a moment, I considered sending them through the jungle back to where they had come from, but my spirit dissuaded me from said impulse. Instead, I allowed them to stay with us in our spacious bohíos to spend the night, claiming it would be safer to return only after Boinayel left his cave, thus guiding them in the treading of their path. Koló could not thank me enough for our demonstrations of peace. Whereas some of his men preferred to sleep in beddings made of palm leaves, others, the Guanahani naboria so confessed, were now growing so accustomed to the hámacas they did not wish to lie down on the floor ever again, no matter what they put between them and the surface'.

Chapter XI
Feliz Navidad

Between Columbus's finding of San Salvador on the night of the eleventh day of October and the early hours of the twelfth, in the year of Our Lord fourteen hundred ninety-two, and the landfall in the mound that turned out to be his major treasure trove in his entire journey, christened «La Isla Española», fifty-five days came to pass.

Concerning Martín Alonso and Francisco Martín Pinzón's Pinta, there was nothing new to report; ever since her disappearance on November the twenty-first, she was still nowhere to be found, likely on her way across the Ocean Sea, headed for Spain, where the Captain and the shipmaster would be paraded throughout the country as the heroes of the West Indies, acclaimed like so by Their Majesties Queen Isabella of Castile and King Fernando II of Aragon. The thought of losing the race to the Far East via West to both those men had been consuming the Admiral ever since Yáñez Pinzón's suggestion that his backstabbing brothers might just come around to doing that, leaving the youngest to the care of the naturalized Spaniard, as if the latter were the former's brand-new father figure.

Then again, what was still keeping Columbus at bay was the thought that, given the date of the Pinta's departure, they had not yet found anything worth showing the Catholic Monarchs; it had been only a fortnight later, in the beginning of December, that the Admiral and the Captain of the Niña signed a mutually lucrative agreement with one of the chieftains of the Taíno, Guacanagaríx, him too willing to make friends with the rulers of Spain and, who knows, acquire some new allies with more powerful weaponry that could put his enemies in their rightful place, achieving peace at last, which is a rather interesting perspective that eventually bringing human beings together all over the world, regardless of having been born and raised in completely different settings and environments, believing of totally opposite religious doctrines, accustomed to greatly unrelated traditions and ways of life, bearing either darker or lighter skin tones,

Columbia: Part I

in short, prejudiced of each other because of all these divergences, only to be joined in the end by the taste for assertion of dominance over those they agree to be of an inferior strain, and that is the one aspect bearing promising results of a highly developed civilization – war. The problem about war, though, is that it is ongoing; it never really comes to an end, for the first attack necessarily demands retribution, a cycle that never breaks – not even when the necessary resources to keep on battling come to an end, an event that constitutes nothing more than a hiatus allowing the losing side to quickly rebuild their strength and double the impact, catching the winning side by surprise, growing more nervous day by day, until the other faction makes a mistake from overconfidence and starts losing all over again. It is in the nature of conflicts to feed on people's bloodthirst, so it is really no wonder they never die out. Unfortunately for Guacanagaríx, though, those were the white leader's thoughts as far as the chieftain himself and his people were concerned. That is what friends are for, after all – we keep them until we need them, then get rid of them when we are fine on our own, sentenced to dying alone by the cosmos, for lack of a better vocable (as "god" is a breaking point in itself).

The truth is (for the time being, at least) things were going well aboard La Gallega and the Niña.

Scouting of other areas off the coast of La Española (for short) and a few landings elsewhere within the borders of the Cacicazgo of Marién proved to be extraordinarily fruitful, as Columbus and Yáñez Pinzón kept collecting tokens from other villages under the orders of Guacanagaríx, simultaneously assessing the conditions for the building of a settlement, except the remaining Pinzón brother knew nothing of this – the Admiral was secretly trying to think of a way to mark his presence on the island as a backup plan, just in case the Pinta never showed. It was, after all, the likeliest scenario, considering Christmas was on its way, if Columbus' calculations were correct (which they probably were, given his thorough recordkeeping), and neither Martín Alonso nor Francisco Martín Pinzón would have wanted to sail around for much longer. On the other hand, if they were in fact somewhere nearby, then they would have had to collect supplies to stay alive throughout the past month; the question was finding out where they got them from. If the Pinzón brothers happened to have made contact with another cacicazgo and its respective leader, one who could have fallen out of favor with Guacanagaríx, the latter could easily accuse them of distastefully toying with his good will, robbing from the entire island while pretending to be friends with one cacique after the other, supporting them all in their causes against the others.

Columbia: Part I

As was the case every time the Kalinago sought to invade La Española, the island's five caciques eventually presented a united front, coming to an internal truce, and kicked the invaders out with a great deal more effectiveness. If the invaders turned out to be the Spaniards, there is no guarantee the chieftains would not behave the same way and attempt to kill every last white man, which means Columbus needed to tread carefully, as these "indios" were not as underdeveloped as all the others he had found along the way. The way the Taíno society of La Española's Cacicazgo of Marién worked was remarkable; while Guacanagaríx seemed to have been under the impression the Admiral had been a tad disrespectful toward him and his people, mostly because of their religious beliefs and the associated dancing rituals, Columbus was in fact jealous of the groundbreaking manner with which the cacique ruled what the Admiral thought were reasonless "beasts".

Despite the obvious differences between nitaínos, bohiques, and naborias, which were very much the equivalent of European nobility, clergy, and populace, respectively, the implemented system worked for everyone; the confederation of "yucayeques", which was what they called their villages, only empowered the cacique's right to govern, and from the maternal side of their lineage, no less, meaning that women played an incredibly important role as far as internally maintaining the cacicazgos together was concerned. The chieftains' families marked their presence all over, especially through marital ties, given the rulers' right to have as many wives as they desired, not necessarily meaning they had to wed a woman per settlement.

The rate of speed at which resources were transubstantiated into all sorts of goods, ranging from perishables to textiles, idolatry objects, musical instruments, jewelry, spices (even hotter than those in the Europeans' possession), the development level of warfare, the cornucopian abundance of crops the soils yielded all year round, the not so pleasantly hot weather tempered with mild tropical rain for the refreshment of the people and the renewal of nature as created by their primordial goddess "Atabey", the willingness of the people to contribute to their cohabitants' well-being without ever protesting against superior orders (because the cacique made sure everyone was fed accordingly, despite their social stratus)… all of this had only taken Columbus's dream a few stories higher, as this was not just about getting settled for life or having his name immortalized through millennia to come anymore, no – now, this was about having a kingdom of his own. The only way he could accomplish something like that, however, was to recruit other Spaniards by the hundreds and not just dozens, carrying with them all the necessary tools and, more importantly, heavy artillery with which to subjugate the marvel of the Taíno to, more than Spanish, Christian domain, as was the Admiral's right while he played the role of an impromptu missionary. Columbus had no choice but to return to Europe; he wanted to see his children again, Beatriz, claim the reward offered by the Catholic Monarchs on her behalf, find his brothers, Giácomo and Bartholomew, and appoint them adelantados, a co-governor position entitling them to handle their big brother's affairs in his absence. The most important reason, however, seemed to be his desire to come back as soon as possible and take over the system for himself, allowing his ambition to get in the way of true Christian values.

***

By the time Christmas Eve was over and the early hours of December twenty-fifth were only just starting, after everyone went to sleep with a full stomach in celebration of the birth of Our Lord, thus taking a break from attentive vigilance, Columbus conspired with his master-at-arms, Diego de Arana (who was also a sort of father-in-law figure to the Admiral, even though the latter was considerably older) in his cabin, with the lights out, waiting for those on deck to be out for the count after having had a generous serving of yuca beer under Columbus's authority and with Guacanagaríx's blessing, the one who had made the offer.

It did not take long for the sailors, cozied up in their «hámacas», feeling warm both on the inside and out (due to the fermentation and the climate, respectively) to start snoring up toward the starry sky, where the Admiral was sure God Almighty was watching, encouraging him to move ahead with his plans. Diego de Arana, however, was not so sure about lighting the fuse of yet another ruse:

'Are you sure we should be doing this, Cristóbal…? If only you would just plead with the men that…', but he was interrupted by Columbus, peeking from behind the slightly ajar cabin door.

'Diego, listen to me – these men are beyond exhausted, they don't want to be here, and they certainly don't want to not be able to choose between heading back and having to stay a while longer, savvy? We need to create a diversion that'll make them believe someone among them is careless and guilty at the same time – preferably someone other than you or myself. Look, I'll leave you in charge of the settlement, sail away as fast as the wind takes us, and then come back the moment the Queen awards me the biggest fleet Man has ever seen, all ships equipped with everything and everyone we need to start turning this place upside-down and build our own little kingdom, away from all the peer pressure of European nobility.

Columbia: Part I

You'll officially be acknowledged co-governor and, once we're all set here, I'll bring Beatriz and the children with me, one happy family in charge of the entire island, not just portions like the ones the indios have now – we need access to the whole place if we're going to make the best out of it, and the lineage will keep on going until Judgment Day, when the Lord shall reward us with an eternal afterlife in Heaven'.

We remember how easily the Admiral's oratory skills would convince pretty much anybody, but when it came to people with a much closer link to him, which was definitely Arana's case (not to mention somewhat of a weakmindedness), thinking twice was usually expendable, except he had just one more question prior to confirming he was in:

'How will I assert my authority…? I've already told you what they were like to me when you were locked in here. Putting me in charge and then leaving won't hold them in their rightful place for too long… they might even kill me…'.

'Don't worry about it!', Columbus exclaimed, further explaining, 'The plan is simple – the wind is already in our favor, the ship is facing the right way, and we don't even need to unfurl the sails; all we need is to quietly lift the anchor from the seabed and the undulation alone will run the vessel aground. When it does, you'll already be in the forecastle, whereas I will remain here. Once everyone realizes what's happening, you come out and admonish them fiercely. They'll get all confused... it'll be chaotic, and that's when you'll come back out sounding surprised, trying your best to find the culprit. Since we know it's no one's fault, none of them will be punished, but you'll keep a close watch either way. Make sure your scabbard is visible and you have a harquebus at the ready on your back. After that, we abandon ship and it's done'.

Arana, also peeking from behind the cabin door, looked the Admiral in his eyes and finally said, with a bit of a smile flourishing from the center of his lips:

'All right... let's do it'.

After a while, walking across the midships section and trying to be as careful as possible not to trip on anyone or anything, both men approached the bow and, together, untied the knot holding the line in place and began pulling. As they did so, the soundtrack immediately behind and above kept playing several tunes, merging all snoring sounds into one far too unpleasant symphony; let us just say the meaning of the original Greek word did not mirror a concord of sound in this particular case at all – except maybe for the fact the whole choir was dissonantly out of tune.

Nevertheless, and every once in a while, the sound would suddenly die out at several points simultaneously, scaring Diego de Arana immensely, who kept looking everywhere trying to find out if anyone was awake and ogling them, only further delaying the unmooring, despite Columbus' sharp whispers:

'Calm down, man! We're wasting time, here! Just keep pulling – the quicker we get this over with, the sooner we'll leave'.

With only a few more feet of line to go, the men heaved as hard as they could and the anchor eventually resurfaced, which was the moment Columbus told his mate to go slower because of the heavy dripping raining on the aquatic surface.

'All right, that's enough. Now let's tie it up and…', the Admiral said in a lower register as he finished performing the required knotting operation, completing his remark with, '… that's that. Now we wait'.

And so it was, with the anchor secured above the water, that the master-at-arms immediately hid inside the forecastle, only a couple of steps away, while the Admiral quietly returned to the cabin on the opposite side and gently closed the door after taking one last peek to ensure there were no witnesses among the mariners to rat him out on his deception. Then again, there was the question of having others aboard apart from sailors.

With the presence of the Moon in the sky, the undulation bore a great deal more strength than on clear nights, moving La Gallega faster toward the shore and further away from the Niña. Columbus could not wait to destroy the largest ship of the flotilla and force a few men to stay behind until his return; the vessel was not his, so he did not care what happened to it. The real owner was still in the cargo hold, manacled to the ship's main mast with several other men awaiting trial after being charged with high treason. They had not bathed in nearly three months, there was only a bucket to split between them all for their bladder and bowel movements (emptied after being filled to the top and then some), their chains allowed little to no motion (for which reason their bodies were probably covered in ulcers from the waste and the chaffing of the wrists on iron), darkness was constant, and the stench was, according to Pedro de Terreros, cabin's boy and the one responsible for feeding the prisoners, mortifyingly foul. Some people could claim that was no legitimate way to treat a fellow countryman, regardless of what they might have done, but about four thousand miles across the Ocean Sea, the African slaves were undergoing an even worse treatment, without any buckets nearby or food, provided only every other day, based on the leftovers of the crews. In short, and judging from the shape they were probably in, if they had to die before reaching Spain, it would not be an issue. Perhaps the Kalinago could find, boil, and eat them

Columbia: Part I

before rotting any more than they already had. The Admiral was sure even someone as sensitive as Sánchez would agree, after having been placed under arrest exactly where the assailants were (except the first had spent only a few hours there, whereas the latter were now closing in on the ninety-day mark).

After a few minutes, both the Admiral and the master-at-arms felt the keel of La Gallega burying itself progressively deeper into the soft plain off the coast of La Española, not far away from Guacanagaríx's village, making the vessel tremble from bow to stern with the force of impact, only made stronger because of the ship's tonnage. The friction of wood and sand made a harsh noise as the waters kept pushing the Santa María further ashore, waking up everyone to a sensation of horror and incredulity which, in turn, drove the sailors into an active trance of panic and confusion, screaming and yelling having erupted all around, even more so once the ship threatened to capsize, vehemently listing to port. Realizing it was time to play his designated role, Diego de Arana pretended he was just getting up from his «hámaca» in the forecastle as the other officers were still unsure of what was happening, thinking it was all but a nightmare.

'Dios mío, what fresh hell is this?!', Pedro de Gutiérrez inquired.

'I don't know!', Escobedo exclaimed, adding,

'The ship just started dragging all of a sudden and nearly tipped over! Master Diego, have you any idea what's going on?!'.

'No, señor, but I'm about to! Someone should've been keeping watch, but I don't think they've done pretty good job about it!', Arana replied in an odd tone the others would have clearly identified as being both premeditated and poorly rehearsed under normal circumstances.

'Well, if that's the case, then I too wish to know who's responsible!', Sánchez intervened, jumping from an aligned «hámaca» to a steep deck floor, which made him slide against the ship wall; if the door had been placed there, he would have been projected straight into the water.

In the cabin, Columbus was holding on to his bed, hoping it would be heavy enough to counter the sliding descent. The Admiral wanted to provide the master-at-arms a little more time to get the situation under control all on his own. As for the Niña's reaction, none was actually produced until Diego de Arana made sure everyone heard him after attempting to draw the sailors' attention:

'Ex-excuse me... please... if I could just... hello...? Gentle-Gentlemen, listen up... please...'.

Enraged because of the continued disrespect the men kept showing him, not just on account of the panic of the present situation, but throughout the entire expedition, the master-at-arms aimed his harquebus at the stars and fired, the sound of the explosion inside the barrel echoing far enough to reach the vessel captained by Vicente Yáñez Pinzón.

'THAT'S IT! I've had it with you scurvy-riddled seadog pissants! I am the master-at-arms, I am second in command! You either obey the Admiral, me, or both! Little loudmouth sons of biscuit eaters...! Not once you've shown me respect since we left Spain – not once! But it's over, do you hear me?! It-is-OVER! Now, then! I want to know who was responsible for dropping anchor and didn't. Well?! Who was it?! Nobody, huh...? It must've been me, I suppose...! That's why I left it on deck! Because I didn't feel like casting it onto the seabed, where it belongs whenever we're not sailing!'.

Silence had become ominously prevalent. Since no one dared speak, not only because the men did not know who was to blame, but most importantly because they did not want to upset the master-at-arms any more than he already was, the latter proceeded:

'Very well, then. Since it's obviously no one's fault we've just lost our flagship to the coast, here's what's going to happen – every man will start salvaging and recovering everything he can carry ashore and come back to help the others the very moment the Sun comes up! Make sure you don't drop anything important, especially the tributes the chieftain gave us, or so help me God, I will hand you over to the canibales myself! Savvy?! Now get on with it! Away with ye!'.

As Diego de Arana finally unstoppered the blaze that had been wildly growing inside him since the first day of the expedition, meeting the gaze of every man he could find, so did they look him in the eye, rendered astonished, dumbfounded, and flabbergasted, all of these synonymous with each other, but still not enough to describe the crew's reaction to the master-at-arms' new side, one he had apparently been hiding under the thick layer of a mousy little man, shedding it off at last.

Columbus, who had been watching from the cabin's veering doorway, was too left amazed at how his only family on that side of the world was grabbing the bulls by the horns. He cleared his throat to make himself heard and, after having everyone simultaneously look at him like a flock of trained birds, including Arana, said:

'Well… you've heard the boss. The ship's lost, so… let her be and we get to it in the morning'.

And so they did. Not far behind, the Niña was moving to the closest point she could get to without suffering the same fate, though she was a lot easier to maneuver on shallow waters because of her carrack features. Yáñez Pinzón could be spotted by the forepeak, calling out on Columbus:

'Almirante! Almirante!'.

Columbia: Part I

The Admiral then let himself slide toward the staircase connecting the quarterdeck and the poop deck, leaning from it to see and talk to the Captain of the Niña:

'Ah!, Pinzón… a rather unfortunate accident, I'm afraid. It seems like someone forgot to drop anchor – can you believe it…? All this time dropping and unmooring, and this is how it ended'.

'Really…? Nobody dropped anchor? Funny… I could swear I'd heard both yours and ours being dropped almost at the same time… I guess I was wrong', Yáñez Pinzón stated.

'Clearly… it's right there, can you see it? In a knot', Columbus casually said, pointing to his concealed brilliance.

'I must say, Colón… I find your good humor surprisingly unaffected. This is the flagship, after all… in fact, more importantly, how will we make it out of here now? There's not enough room aboard for both your crew and mine', Yáñez Pinzón remarked.

'True, Pinzón, true… nevertheless, before we head back to Spain, I intend to scout for your brothers and split the men proportionately between the Niña and the Pinta', Columbus explained.

'Yes, but… even if you do that, it'll still be too crowded', the Captain noticed.

Wishing Yáñez Pinzón would just let it go,

which apparently he did not feel like doing, the Admiral sought to quickly dismiss the subject, much to the Captain's increasing suspicions of foul play:

'One problem at a time, Pinzón. All right? One problem at a time. First, we deal with the wreckage and salvage as much as possible. Then... we figure out the math'.

'Very well... as you wish, Almirante...', Yáñez Pinzón said, willing to wager Columbus definitely had something to do with the loss of La Gallega.

***

Come the morning, the crews of both the disgraced Santa María and the sleek Niña combined their strength and took ashore all riches they had collected since making landfall in San Salvador. With the only remaining ship secured beyond doubt, as per Yáñez Pinzón's insistence, some of the men stayed on the beach to look out for their possessions, inclusively getting help from the boarding natives, and all of their own accord, an attitude the Admiral applauded before taking with him a couple of their friends picked up from other islands to Guacanagaríx's village, leaving the inflated Diego de Arana in charge so as to keep practicing his newly-found ironfisted governing skills. When Yáñez Pinzón asked Columbus where he was going as he entered the jungle accompanied,

Columbia: Part I

however, the Admiral pretended he was already out of earshot and had not been able to hear.

A few hours later, Columbus and his small party reached their destination and, as always, he was greeted with extraordinary amicability from all villagers, regardless of their being nitaínos, behiques, or naboria; the one who gladly had him over at his own grand bohío was, of course, the cacique himself.

The Admiral was relying on his indigenous company's Castilian skills, as limited as they might have been, to understand what he wanted to ask Guacanagaríx and then relay the message in the idiom they shared. Columbus thus requested the cacique allow the construction of a small fort where a few of his men could stay during his voyage back to the «Old World», considering the disaster endured not many hours before.

'Disaster...?', Guacanagaríx inquired, adding, 'What happened?'.

Having translated both questions to broken Castilian, Columbus provided the cacique his version of the tragedy, which the natives accompanying him reverted to Taíno. Taking advantage of the fact the Admiral was not at all fluent in their language, the youths paused several times, pretending to be looking for the proper words when they were actually explaining what they had seen with their own eyes:

'He and another white man waited for everyone to fall asleep, unhooked the barge from the reef, and let the waters bring the ship ashore. We believe they did it on purpose, just so they could leave their people behind and start spreading roots into your grounds, O Great Cacique'.

Columbus kept averting his gaze from the natives he had in his custody to Guacanagarix, unable to make out the words, but looking, nevertheless, for a hint based on the chieftain's expression. As the youths shared their theory, the cacique gave the Admiral a side-look, but he did not make it too long, in order to protect his own kin.

'Very well', the chieftain said, 'you have my permission to erect your bohío in the outskirts of our yucayeque. My people will aid your men in any way they can regarding their subsistence, but I do ask they hold an end of their own in this deal and provide a helping hand. No one living in my domain remains idle'.

After getting the gist of the cacique's words, Columbus replied:

'Of course, Your Excellency! Thank you, thank you very much; I appreciate your kindness and good will. It shall be done'.

The Admiral bowed to the cacique in reverence, who, in turn, mirrored the white man's gesture. Guacanagarix then turned to his fellow locals and gave them a set of instructions:

Columbia: Part I

'If you wish to stay with the white man Koló, let no one stop you and farewell across the seas to his domain. However, if you no longer desire to remain in his presence and have no intention of following him, then be sure to make yourselves scarce halfway through the jungle and turn left toward the Guanarawi. Tell whoever you find there fishing that Guacanagaríx sent and authorized you to take a kanoa for you to return to your land'.

The youths agreed and thanked the chieftain. In turn, Columbus waited a few seconds for the translation, which was taking its sweet time to come. He then had to ask:

'Well? What did he say?'.

The natives had already forgotten about the Admiral, hence their delay. They did, nevertheless, come up with the best story they could to fool him, telling him the cacique had asked them if they were thinking of leaving with him and the other whites, to which they had replied affirmatively, eager to embrace the «Old World» as their version of Paradise.

'Oh!... I'm happy to hear it', Columbus said, apparently unsuspicious of the truth.

A few moments later, the Admiral was offered a morning meal to help him return to where he planned to build the settlement replenished.

Repeatedly evidencing his gratitude for the chieftain's good graces, Columbus left with the youths back to the beach where the Santa María had run aground. On a chart, both spots would probably seem quite close to each other, but it was walking through the jungle, averting the vegetation, and watching out for any life-threatening creatures that made the trail much longer.

After a while, the Admiral, still digesting his breakfast, leaned on a tree and asked the "indios" to wait as he caught his breath back. They told him, however, they only wanted to scout a bit more to make sure no snakes attacked him when he walked by, adding they would call him once they saw it was all clear.

Columbus saw them move calmly and had no reason to suspect they were in fact looking for an auspicious moment to flee. It was only a few moments afterward that the foliage of the bushes and the shrubs stopped sounding like they were being pushed away, prompting the Admiral to call out for the natives:

'Hello? Are you there...? Is it okay to advance or what...?!', but no response was uttered.

Relatively capable of resuming his treading, Columbus moved to the spot where he had last seen the youths and called out again, but silence remained predominant, apart from a few squawks projected by the birds, mainly parrots.

'Why, the little savages... I guess they're much smarter than they care to make it look... all the more reason to get these beasts under control as quickly as possible, and nothing like keeping an eye on them starting today, which, now that I remember, is Christmas... hmm... that gives me an idea', the Admiral said out loud, talking to himself, no doubt, for his landing party was by then closing in on the river, hoping to paddle home and escape the clenches of the white men who, so it seemed, had nothing to do with Paradise, rather looking to bring chaos to an otherwise peaceful and perfectly functioning world that could do well without the presence of the dead-colored from hell.

* * *

'Get on with it, now – don't drop anything!', Diego de Arana kept telling the men, pacing on the beach with his harquebus unholstered and the grip of his sword just a few inches away from being quickly sheathed out of its scabbard.

This whole side of the master-at-arms was, of course, quite a novelty that had impressed the sailors enough into showing him the respect he thought he deserved, considering his position in the chain of command. Like all tyrants, however, their rule does not last long, for the people eventually grow tired of being bossed around the clock and treated like scum; it is only when the tables turn that they do not mind doing the same to others, sparking, therefore, the ongoing internal retribution cycle. If anyone were to ask what is worse, fighting each other or joining forces to fight a different group entirely, the answer they would get would most likely be rather dubious and moralistic, of course, especially when coming from men dubbed "spiritual", acknowledging the need for "holy wars"; conversion by force is the Christian way to go, but that is a story for another time.

Making his way from the Niña on said vessel's rowboat to the keeled Santa María, Yáñez Pinzón was directly transferring certain goods that would be better off aboard the carrack, where it was safer. As he approached, he heard the clank of chains from inside the hull, realizing someone was in there. The Captain knew who they were – he simply had forgotten all about them, pretty much like everyone else. Still, he cried through the boards, hoping to successfully relay his message:

'Are you all right in there?'.

An intensified clanking sound made itself heard and someone was definitely screaming as loud as they could, though the words were quite unclear. Yáñez Pinzón was considering going inside, but he did not have any means at his disposal to release the prisoners. Also, he did not know whether Columbus agreed to the thought, let alone the decision. He had been in command of that ship, after all, so it was up to him.

Columbia: Part I

Fortunately, the Captain of the Niña did not have to debate himself in his mind for too long, considering the Admiral appeared from behind the trees only a few moments later. Yáñez Pinzón then took advantage of that cue and rowed toward the beach. Once he jumped out of the rowboat and into to the clear, shallow waters, he addressed Columbus and asked:

'May I ask where you've been to, Almirante? You look a wee bit... ravaged. What happened?'.

Taking a deep breath, Columbus sat down and leaned his back on the trunk of a tree, saying:

'Well... it turns out my company decided to leave about halfway back and... I had to retrace my steps all by myself, but no matter – it's fine, now. So, how are the salvaging operations going?'.

'Fine. Your master-at-arms seems to have the hand of things... I'm just not so sure he should be pushing the crew too hard, especially those who never cared much for him, but... it's every man for himself, isn't it?', Yáñez Pinzón remarked.

Columbus stared at the Captain for a while, the meaning of his words rather unclear to him, though he eventually decided not to pursue the subject. Still, Yáñez Pinzón proceeded, as he wished to tell the Admiral about the prisoners' situation:

'Colón, I was just rowing by La Gallega and heard the men you imprisoned crying out for help.

You're not leaving them there to die, are you?'.

Columbus averted his gaze from the Captain's and ogled the totaled vessel, simultaneously commenting with a stern expression on his face:

'I don't know... maybe I should, but if I did, I wouldn't be allowing Justice to take its due course, now would I? I want Their Majesties to know about this and have the Holy Tribunal deal with them. We'll take them out of there in a moment, get them in shipshape and put them in the Niña's hold. Nobody should ever get away with murder, Pinzón – nobody'.

Speaking of removing the prisoners from the wreckage of La Gallega, Columbus got up again, put his hand on Yáñez Pinzón's shoulder and walked past him, addressing everyone on the beach and calling all others working on the vessel.

'Caballeros, I have a bit of news for you all. During my short absence, I went to meet with the chieftain of the village we've all been to several times and... I asked him for permission to build a fort right behind these trees, where we can stay lodged until we bring back more resources from Spain to develop a small town and start earning a living, especially from the gold these indios keep hiding from us. The gifts we've been collecting so far indicate there's a lot to be mined – possibly all over the island; however, and until we mingle with these people on a permanent basis, we won't have earned their trust enough to let us walk about and do our work properly. Having said that, I must now ask of you something very much important in order for this project to be fruitful – who here is willing to stay behind, build a fort from that wreckage there, open our first settlement in India, and watch over it?'.

Yáñez Pinzón's suspicions had just been confirmed – the wreckage had indeed been deliberate. Columbus wanted to leave his influence on the island so he could come back to an even friendlier environment, hopefully under the subjugation of the Spanish.

As for the men, however, they did not seem too keen on the idea. They looked at each other and looked inside themselves, weighing the pros and cons of staying in a place that was gravely hot, humid, primitive, unpleasant in general, but where they could also go rogue and show disregard for laws neither the island nor its people had ever heard about, living as they very well pleased, perhaps even rejoicing over the fact they would be the first to collect a nice amount of gold for themselves, keeping it hidden from Columbus' sight whenever he returned, claiming they had found no mines whatsoever. It was a dastardly cunning plan. Who would keep track of their actions, anyway?

And so it was that, to the Admiral's surprise, a little over thirty-five men volunteered to stay and build the fort from the Santa María's timber.

'Well done… I congratulate you for your bravery! Know that I shall inform Their Majesties of your decision and recommend that you be commended for it. Don Rodrigo, if you will please join me and take note that, on Christmas Day of the year of Our Lord fourteen hundred ninety-two, the Expedition of Great Admiral Cristóbal Colón to India Beyond the Ganges suffered the misfortune of losing a caravel to the reefs of La Española, nevertheless compensating such loss with the reuse of said vessel's timber to establish the very first European settlement in the New World per God's great grace and on behalf of Their Most Serene Majesties, our patrons, christened, because of today's symbology, «La Navidad», complemented by its natural harbor, «Puerto de la Navidad». Let it also be known that, in charge of the settlement, I leave Master Diego de Arana, appointed Chief Constable, and Mayordomo Pedro de Gutiérrez and Secretary Rodrigo de Escobedo as his aids'.

Having only then heard who the governing body of the settlement was comprised of, some of the volunteers felt a little unease assaulting the integrity of their chest, also looking down to their feet to avoid facing the master-at-arms, grateful to Columbus for the nomination as if it were the first time he had heard about it. The die was now cast, and each plank the crew took from La Gallega meant they were one step closer to finally assess first-hand what it was like to bring the European concept of civilization to the earthly Garden of Eden.

Chapter XII
Sling Your Hook

The year of Our Lord fourteen hundred ninety-three was off to a good start for the Columbian Expedition to India Beyond the Ganges. All that uncertainty of three months before now sounded irrelevant to even hold in the voyage's records. The Great Admiral of the Fleet and the Ocean Sea Christopher Columbus had promised and eventually delivered – the seaway to the Far East was a reality, and all because of the Genoa-born Spanish navigator's persistence, whose competence and eloquence had also greatly contributed to the finding of a route that would make other European kingdoms tear their charts apart out of green-eyed jealousy, for Their Majesties the Queen of Castile and the King of Aragon were the sole and rightful proprietors of the trading course at hand, one whose tolls promised to make the Spanish Crown's pockets heavier than ever.

Columbus only dreamed of the reception he would be given by the Catholic Monarchs, forever immortalized as the greatest explorer of all time, perhaps even greater than his own idol, Marco "Il Milione" Polo.

Ahead of him and part of his crew, combined with the original sailors of the Niña, on which he was now aboard and of which he split command with Yáñez Pinzón to avoid the same sort of confrontation he had experienced with Juan de la Cosa, chained in the hull below with the other traitors, another month and a half worth of a return leg awaited, God knows with how many storms to face along the way.

On the beach of the newly-founded La Navidad, on January fourth, the thirty-six men who had volunteered to stay behind, among which were calkers, James Wardropper, the Lord of the Wardrobes, Juan Sánchez, the doctor, gunners, carpenters (including Antonio de Cuéllar), and Luis de Torres, the interpreter, together with the three governors, Chief Constable Diego de Arana, Secretary Rodrigo de Escobedo, and Mayordomo Pedro de Gutiérrez, waved their goodbyes to the eastbound Niña, which was to harbor a few more villagers

Columbia: Part I

along the coast of La Española, taken by force to Spain, where they would be displayed in front of the Catholic Monarchs like the exotic animals the Spanish already had in their possession.

Two days later, on the sixth and incoming from the North, the Pinta was sighted at last, having received orders from the implacable Admiral to come by the side, allowing him and Vicente Yáñez to board her and confront both Martín Alonso and Francisco Martín Pinzón. The argument at hand comprised a great deal of insults and accusations exchanged between the four men whose nature we have already learned about and will not, therefore, reproduce. Suffice it to say the youngest Pinzón brother felt hurt for quite a long time into the journey before he could forgive his family, whereas Columbus, not so benevolent, spent most of his time inking a highly detailed descriptive letter on which he reported the events endured since August last, not just concerning the marvels he had found and claimed for the Crown, but also pointing fingers at innumerous other people he intended to bring before Justice as retribution, precisely, for what could have been, in his opinion, a rather peaceful voyage whose purpose he had eventually fulfilled, for such was the will of Our Lord, having become, instead, an immensely perilous journey he had no intention of living through again, as his mission for the near future was far nobler – serve God, Their Majesties, his patrons, and Mankind by returning to La Española, where the Great Admiral of the Fleet and the Ocean Sea, Viceroy and Governor-General of the West Indies was bound to spread the One Faith all across the land and build his own empire, generating a Columbian dynasty whose first heir apparent was Diogo Columbus and would perdure the hand of time for centuries to come.

To be continued…

Biography

Tiago Lameiras was born in Lisbon, Portugal, in 1990. He holds a Bachelor's Degree with Honors in Theater – Acting, from the Higher School of Theater and Film of Lisbon. He is presently completing his doctoral thesis in Communications, Culture, and Arts – Cultural Studies Specialization, at the School of Arts and Humanities of the University of the Algarve, Faro, Portugal.

His titles are comprised of: *Portvcale – A Epopeia Portuguesa da Contemporaneidade* (2010), *Viagem ao Centro de Ti – Romance Trovado* (2012), *A Mão de Diónisos* (2013), *Actor Being: A Role in Mankind, Utopian Ambition: Constitution of the 2100 Atlantian Republic* (2016), *Sonata, Epistulæ* (2017), *Persephone's Fall* (2018), and *Hypatia: Empress of Alexandria* (2019).

Printed in Great Britain
by Amazon